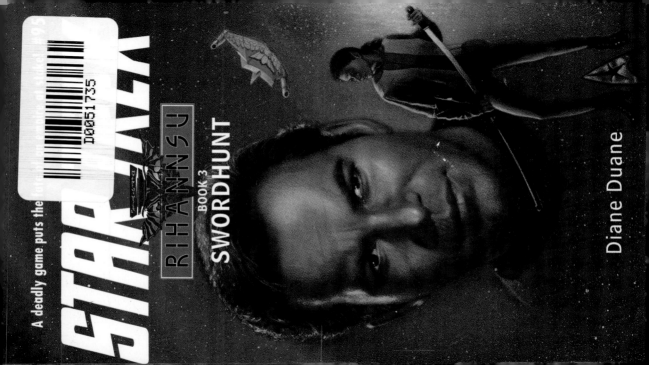

STAR TREK

A deadly game puts the fate of an entire empire at stake! #9.5

D0051735

RIHANNSU

BOOK 3

SWORDHUNT

Diane Duane

$6.99 U.S.
$9.99 CAN.

ISBN 0-671-04209-2

EAN

"EIGHTEEN SECONDS, CAPTAIN."

It felt like eighteen years. "Preparing for warp eleven," Sulu said. "Accelerating out of the gravity well now."

"Back in a moment, *Bloodwing*," Jim said. The ship was cooling again, but that would not last. Out they went into the dark, and three of the seven ships came after them.

"Warp two. Warp three. Pursuit is in warp and accelerating."

"Ready on the aft phaser banks, Mr. Chekov. Prepare a spread of torpedoes."

"Ready, Captain."

"Warp five," Sulu said. "Warp six. Turning." Everything slewed sideways: the ship was groaning softly now, the skinfield complaining about the stresses being applied to it . . . and worse was to come.

"Aft view," Jim said. The screen flickered. Jim saw two of the pursuing Romulan vessels trying to turn to match, but not doing as well: turning wide, losing ground. The third one, the biggest of them, was turning and gaining on them, and firing.

"Clean misses. Warp eight," Sulu said. Suddenly 15 Trianguli was swelling to fill the screen, flashing toward them. "Warp nine——"

"Mind that helm, mister," Jim said softly.

"Warp ten. She's steady, Captain," Sulu said, while the ship began to shake and her structural members to howl in a way that suggested Sulu's definition of *steady* was a novel one. "High photosphere. Warp eleven!"

STAR TREK®: RIHANNSU
By Diane Duane

#1: *My Enemy, My Ally*
#2: *The Romulan Way (with Peter Morwood)*
#3: *Swordhunt*
#4: *Honor Blade*

STAR TREK®

RIHANNSU

BOOK 3
SWORDHUNT

Diane Duane

POCKET BOOKS
New York London Toronto Sydney Singapore

This book is a work of fiction. Names, characters, places and incidents are products of the author's imagination or are used fictitiously. Any resemblance to actual events or locales or persons, living or dead, is entirely coincidental.

An *Original* Publication of POCKET BOOKS

POCKET BOOKS, a division of Simon & Schuster, Inc.
1230 Avenue of the Americas, New York, NY 10020

Copyright © 2000 by Paramount Pictures. All Rights Reserved.

A VIACOM COMPANY

STAR TREK is a Registered Trademark of Paramount Pictures.

This book is published by Pocket Books, a division of Simon & Schuster, Inc., under exclusive license from Paramount Pictures.

ISBN: 0-671-04209-2

First Pocket Books printing October 2000

10 9 8 7 6 5 4 3 2 1

POCKET and colophon are registered trademarks of Simon & Schuster, Inc.

Printed in the U.S.A.

For Wilma, T.R. and Sara,
who saw all this begin
in the House of the Dangerously Single Women
. . . and for Wes, Lee, Gene and Peter,
who left us all much less Single
(though no less Dangerous)

Editor's Note

In the days before *Star Trek: The Next Generation* came to the air and provided definitive information about the inhabitants of the Federation, their backgrounds and interactions, Pocket Books published several novels that speculated on the cultures and habits of alien species such as the Klingons and Romulans. Two of the most popular titles were *My Enemy, My Ally* and *The Romulan Way*, both of which focused on Romulan society. Although *The Next Generation* and its televised successors ultimately took Romulan culture in a different direction, fan interest in the Rihannsu, as Diane Duane described them, has remained strong throughout the years. This special series, which is meant to stand apart from established *Star Trek* continuity, continues the author's speculation on the intricate fabric of Romulan—or, rather, Rihannsu—society.

SWORDHUNT

Prologue

THE SHADOWS of Eilhaunn's little yellow sun Ahadi were slanting low, now, over the pale green fields all around the flitter port, as the work crews ran the harvesting machinery up and down the newly cut rows to bind the reeds into the big circular bales that Hwiamna's family favored. Hwiamna i-Del t'Ehweia stood there off at the margin of the field, watching the two machines that her son and daughter were driving: and she sighed. They were racing again. They loved to race, each challenging the other every morning to do the work better, faster; and whichever one was the victor, on a given day, chaffed the other mercilessly about it until the next daymeal, when there might be another victor, or the same one. Hwiamna routinely prayed the Elements that the victories should alternate; otherwise home life became rather strained.

Hwianna smiled, took off her sun hat, and wiped her brow, while taking a moment to beat some accumulated windblown reed-seed off the hat's thin felt, against her long breeches. Since the twins were born, Kul clutching at Niysa's heel, this kind of thing had been going on; and it would doubtless go on well past the end of the year, when their acceptances came through. Naturally as soon as they were both old enough, they had both applied to the Colleges of the Great Art on ch'Rihan; there being no higher possible goal, to their way of thinking, for anyone born on a colony world so far from the heart of the Empire, with so little else to recommend it. Hwianna was not sure about their assessment—her foremothers on one side of the family had willingly come here three generations ago from the crowded city life of Theijhoi on ch'Havran—and once they had paid off their relocation loan, won their land grant, and tamed the earth to the bearing of regular crops of stolreed, they had found life good here. But farm life, and even the prospect of managing the family flitter port, was not good enough for the new generation. Their eyes were on the stars—which should possibly have been expected, for Hwianna's father was of Ship-Clan blood, native to Eilhaunn for two generations—where Hwianna's eyes were on the ground. She had no doubt whatever that both of the twins would be accepted. Then this rivalry would go on as always, but within the structure of the Colleges, and later on, with appointments to Grand Fleet. Perhaps they would go further, into diplomatic service or the uppermost reaches of Fleet. Knowing her children, Hwiamna had little doubt of that, either. But right now all she could wish was that they would fail to destroy the farm machinery, which had to last for at least a couple of seasons more before it went back to the cooperative for recycling or replacement.

She put her hat back on and walked back over to what she had been inspecting—the piles of firewood carefully stacked up in hand-built racks twenty *rai* from the edges of the flitter port's landing aprons. Hwiamna knew, for she had seen pictures of them, that on the Hearthworlds the ports did not have such: but the images always looked bare to her, and somehow underutilized, as if an opportunity was being missed. Here, out among the Edgeworlds, resources could be scarce enough that no possible energy source could afford to be ignored. The resinous dense wood of ealy, a tree native to Eilhaunn, burnt hot and long; it was excellent for controlled combustion in power stations, and also for the small hearth-fires of the householders in the area. They all helped to cut it—thus keeping the surrounds of the landing aprons clear—and they all helped to stack it in the racks; and each winter season, when the first snows began, all the householders gathered to take away bundles of the dried, cured wood, carefully divided

3

according to how much time they had spent in the work of coppicing and stacking. *The trouble is,* Hwianna thought, looking with some resignation at the racks, *that time alone should not be the only cri- terion by which we judge the division. . . .*

The comm button clipped to her pocket squeaked. "Mother?"

She reached in and touched it. "Kul dear," Hwianna said, "pray, don't pass so close to your brother in the middle of the rows. You're going to make life harder for whoever has to pick up the bales."

"That will be him," Kul said, cheerful, "and it's right that life should be harder for him, if I have any- thing to do with it. But, Mother, we're almost done now; is there anything else needs doing out here be- fore lastmeal?"

"I don't think so, daughter," Hwianna said. "Though I may have some words for the two of you about the way this wood's been stacked. Your super- vision last cutting-day leaves a little to be desired, I think." She turned away from the rack she had been regarding critically.

"Mother," Niysa said, "that wasn't her fault; it was the Droalls. Those people couldn't be troubled to cut their own wood straight, leave alone anyone else's. And they can't be made to do it, either, stand over them how you like. I think you should cut them out of the coppicing rotations in future; they're more trouble than they're worth."

Hwianna sighed, amused. As usual, there was no

upbraiding one of the twins for anything whatsoever without the other coming straight in to his or her defense. "We'll talk about it later," she said; though privately Hwiamna was inclined to agree with her son. "Get yourselves finished, get yourselves in . . ."

"Should I come fetch you, Mother?"

"No, *bhun*, you go on ahead; the walk will do me good. . . ."

She watched one of the machines half an *irai* away finish its row; then both machines made for the unplanted strip at the edge of the field and began racing down it over the slight rise in the ground there and back toward the apron, where their house was built a little ways back from the old road leading to the two low prefabricated cast-stone buildings which the government had installed as the flitter port's administrative center.

Hwiamna gave the wood racks one last look and then began walking back around the edge of the apron toward the house. It had been a good year for the reed, for once; a welcome change from last year, when the growing season had been blighted by endless wet weather and what seemed equally endless uncertainty over what was going on in their region of space. They were a long way out in the Empire. That was one of the reasons it had been so easy for the family to move out all this way, in her grandfather's time. New uncrowded worlds had been as plentiful as birds in the sky; it had seemed then, and the government had been easygoing about relocation finance and support for new colonists. Now, though, people were beginning to realize what the real price for such worlds might be. The government was not so forthcoming with aid anymore, a stance which was starting to cause complaints as the inhabitants of worlds like Eilhaunn began to realize that interplanetary trade and defense were matters they were increasingly expected to manage themselves—though there was notably no talk whatever of excusing them from taxes. It all made for nerve-racking times, as last year, when there had been talk of the government beginning a program of granting the farther-flung outworlds "autonomy": code, Hwianna strongly suspected, for leaving them completely to their own devices.

But that kind of talk seemed to have quieted down since, much to Hwianna's relief. And the weather had settled itself, too. This last season had been nothing but the dry fair weather that was normal for north-continent Eilhaunn-uwe this time of year, and there would be no lack of grain—a relief, for reed was Eilhaunn's great staple, of all the plant foodstuffs the one that grew most readily here. But as usual, the growing was not the end of the business: nothing was guaranteed until the grain was out of the pod and into dry storage.

Hwianna glanced up one more time as she ambled across the landing apron—the habitual gesture this time of year. No one wanted to see cloud moving in when the reed was being cut, since it needed at least a day on the ground in the sun before it could be threshed—otherwise the enzymes in the seed pods would not activate to let the grain loose. Hwiamna scanned the turquoise sky, and breathed out. No cloud.

Yet she squinted into the brightness for a little longer, her curiosity aroused. High up there, very high up, were some thin pale lines of white . . .

Getting less pale, more white.

Not cloud. Contrails.

Hwiamna looked at them and swallowed. The contrails were growing steadily broader toward their arrowy approaching ends. Dropping into atmosphere . . .

Her heart went cold in her side. *The children*, she thought, *where are the children?* For everyone knew what contrails like those meant. The news services had been full of the pictures of them, in the last few months.

Hwiamna started running across the apron. As she ran she missed her footing once, and under her the ground shuddered, faintly at first, then harder. *O Elements,* Hwiamna thought as she ran, *no: not here: why here?!*

And then there was no more time for questions, for over the hills at the edge of the valley came a terrible rumbling, and Hwiamna saw the cruisers come up low and fast over the hills, five of them, firing as they came. She knew the shapes all too well, those long bodies and down-thrust wings and nacelles, like *oiswuh* diving, their long necks thrust forward, the terrible claws out. They too had been in the news

7

services . . . but far away, at what had seemed at the time like a safe distance—

The ships came screaming down and over, and the ground all around the port shuddered as the phaser bolts and photon torpedoes slammed into the fields. Great blooming black-shot clouds of orange fire came boiling up from the impact sites as dirt and rocks shot out from them in all directions, and the biggest one of all from the torpedo that the foremost ship fired into the airport buildings.

Charred and burning wreckage flew, and Hwianna flung herself down on the shaking ground, the air knocked out of her lungs by the force of the explosion. When she struggled up to her knees again, she peered desperately through the smoke and fire to try to make out what was happening. Wind whipped up by the passage of the second and third Klingon cruisers blasted across the apron, pushing the smoke aside for long enough that Hwianna could see someone moving out on the edge of the flitter port, well away from the buildings—Kul, running for one of the flitters.

"Kul!" Hwianna screamed. Then she slapped at the comm button. "Kul! Daughter, no—!"

But her daughter would not listen to her in this, as in most else. She had already slapped the side of the flitter, and the canopy was levering itself up, and Kul was climbing in—

That was when the phaser blast from the next cruiser hit it. Hwianna knelt there frozen as shreds of glittering and burning metal and flesh blasted out from the site. Billowing smoke then veiled the spot where the flitter had stood, but not before Hwianna had seen too much of what preceded the smoke. Her hands clenched together. There was nothing she could do. "Kul . . ." she whispered.

Motion from elsewhere on the apron distracted Hwianna. The other flitter, rising, its engines screaming. "Niysa," she whispered. She would not call him now. If she did, he might be distracted. "Fly, my son, fly for it, get away—!"

It was the last thing on his mind: for he had seen them kill his sister. The flitter was in the air now, and came wrenching around in a high-grav turn that should have pushed the blood right out of his brains; but Niysa was a pilot born, with *neirrh* in his blood, as his instructor had said, and he flew like one of those deadly little birds, racing after the closest of the Klingon cruisers. *He's mad,* Hwianna thought in anguish. *He hasn't enough weaponry to do anything at all—*

But her Niysa did not care, and flung his craft at the cruiser, firing its pitiful little phasers. "No," Hwianna whimpered, for he was actually gaining on the cruiser as it plunged over. Niysa fired, fired again, poured on thrust—

Almost absently the phaser bolt lanced out from the back of the Klingon vessel and touched his ship. It bloomed into fire, vanished in smoke. Lazily the cruiser arced around; and the cloud behind it began to rain splinters and fragments of metal, and lumps of scorched burnt stuff.

Hwianna screamed then, wordlessly, a cry of total horror and grief. The world, all her world, was over, finished, destroyed. Her face streaked with tears of rage and loss, Hwianna stared up into the turquoise sky, now hazed and blackened by the smoke of burning reed, and raised her clenched fists to the heavens, and screamed to the pitiless Elements, "Why?!"

Her only answer was the disruptor bolt that killed her.

Chapter One

DEEP IN the longest night, in a ship passing through the empty space thirteen light-years from 33 Trianguli, a Rihannsu woman sat in a hard-cushioned chair behind a desk and looked out through a small viewport at the stars, waiting.

Her surroundings were blessedly familiar; her own small cabin, in her own ship. It was everything outside, now, which was strange to her—the spaces in which she was a barely tolerated guest, the stars that filled them, either unheeding of her presence or subtly inimical to it. . . .

She raised her eyebrows briefly at her own fancy. *I grow whimsical,* she thought, and her gaze slid sideways from the surface of her tidy desk to the

11

chair which now sat by itself against the far wall. *But perhaps, having you around, there is reason.*

In the present dim nighttime lighting of the cabin, what lay across the arms of the chair seemed barely more than a sliver of shadow; pure unrevealing darkness, absorbing whatever light fell upon it. Not quite straight, but very faintly curved, the sheath and the hilt seeming to fade seamlessly into one another by the skill of the ancient swordsmith, the Sword occupied another empty chair much different from its former one, and the thoughts of the woman whose cabin it now shared.

Occupation . . . She smiled faintly. It was as good a word as any for the hold which this object had had over her since she put her hand out in the Senate chamber, two months and a lifetime ago, to take it. In her people's traditions there had always been tales of creatures or objects which expressed the Elements unusually perfectly. These tended to bend the Universe out of shape around them, as intense gravity fields bend light, and equally they bent awry the intentions of those mortals who had close dealings with them.

She had little thought to find herself, ever, so used. It had simply come to her, in that moment's impulse in the Senate chambers, that she would willingly take possible disaster on herself in order to save the most sacred part of her people's heritage from further dishonor. Now she wondered, sometimes, exactly whose impulse that had been; exactly who was the Sword, and whose were the hand and will wielding it.

In the days following that day, when she and her crew had returned to these spaces where the Federation had allowed them to take refuge, she had spent a number of hours in what was little better than shock—amazement at her own temerity, worry over what would follow it, fear for her crew. Then pragmatism set in, as always, which was as well; for within only a few days more, the messages began to arrive. Her act had swiftly begun to bear fruit in the form of consequences, and the fruit was ripening fast, faster than even she could have imagined.

And soon, now, if she was any judge of events, the first fruit would fall—

The comm signal sounded, and the suddenness of it made her start. She had to laugh at herself, then, though there was no one here to hear except that dark and silent listener lying across the arms of the chair, it wearing its eternal slight uncommunicative smile.

She reached out and touched the control on her desk. *"Ie?"*

"T'Hrienteh says a message has arrived for you in the last comm packet, *llhei.* . . ."

Aidoann's voice had a slight tinge of eagerness to it, and Ael knew whence that eagerness came. All her crew had been infected by it since she came back to *Bloodwing* carrying what now lay on the chair across from her.

"Send it along to my computer," Ael said. "I will

13

read it here. And Aidoann, for the Elements' sake there is little point in *you* 'madam'ing me. The crew will think we have fallen out."

A pause, then a chuckle. "Very well, *ll—Ael*."

"Not in private, anyway," Ael said, hearing her antecenturion's old slight discomfort with amusement, and wondering idly how many years yet it would take her to lose it. "We can afford a little ease among ourselves these days, as long as our performance in action is not impaired. Which I think unlikely to happen. In any case, it is not as if some superior officer is going to come along and reprimand us for a breakdown in discipline."

That image made Aidoann laugh outright. "So," Ael said. "What has tr'Keirianh had to say about the engine tests this morning?"

"He said little, madam," and smiled a great deal."

Ael's mouth quirked up a little at that. Her chief engineer might be sparse of speech, but he had no skill at concealing his feelings. "Dangerous to make assumptions," she said, "but that would seem to bode well. *Ta'khoi . . .*"

As she cut the voice connection, her terminal showed her the herald for an incoming message, encrypted. "Decrypt," she said, and sat back, watching the terminal go black, then fill with amber characters that shimmered into meaning from meaninglessness.

About half the screenful was comm routing information, interesting only insofar as one close to be

14

endlessly fascinated by the means her correspondents found to evade the ever-increasing interest of the security services on ch'Rihan and ch'Havran. Some of the messages were relayed numerous times among the subject worlds of the Empire and right out to the fringes of Rihannsu-dominated space before making their way out into the spaces beyond. This one, she saw, had gone clear out into the Klingon communications networks—which in itself was amusing, considering what one of these messages might eventually mean to the Klingon Empire if things went the way she thought they might—and from there had passed to one of the commercial subspace relay networks in the "nonaligned" worlds buffering between the Klingons and the Federation, before making its way to her ship. *The long way around* . . . she thought, and touched the screen, stroking the routing information away and bringing up the message.

Under the origin and destination fields, both forged, the message itself was brief. The body of it said only:

THE PART YOU HAVE REQUESTED (NTCS 55726935–
7745–9267–93677) IS PRESENTLY UNAVAILABLE.
NEAREST ESTIMATE OF AVAILABILITY IS BETWEEN
THREE TO FIVE MONTHS. IT IS SUGGESTED YOU
SUBSTITUTE PART NTCS 55726935–7456–8344–
86009 AS AN INTERIM SOLUTION. CONTACT US
AGAIN IN THREE STANDARD MONTHS REGARDING
ORIGINAL PART.

There was, of course, no signature. She sat back and looked thoughtfully at the two long "parts numbers," carefully rearranging their digits in her mind according to the usual method . . . then held very still for a few moments, digesting what those two sets of numbers together meant. *So quickly . . .*

She folded her hands again, leaned her chin on them once more, calculating. *They are furious, indeed, for their innate inertia to be so quickly overcome. Yet I cannot believe their consensus is genuine. I have merely given them cause for a show of unity. Beneath that, no question but that their divisions remain.*

Yet will those still run deep enough to serve my turn?

She shifted her eyes back toward the dark, slight curve of the Sword, and felt it looking at her. *Impossible, of course . . .* But the feeling persisted, and others had reported it as well. How something so inanimate could yet seem to have awareness of its surroundings, and an intent that looked out at the world through that awareness, Ael could not tell. Yet for many long years this potent artifact had lain in that chair in the Senate, untouched, unmolested by even the most violent and powerful of the personalities who passed through—and that fact argued some indwelling power of the Sword's more dangerous, in its way, than Ael much liked to think of.

She got up, then; came around her desk, and stood before that chair, looking down at the slice of darkness that lay there defeating the dim light of her cabin. "Well," she said softly. "Now is the time, if ever. Shall we serve each other's turn? I am willing . . ."

She reached out slowly, hesitant; her fingers dropped to the hilt, brushed it . . . Nothing happened; no jolt of power, no arcane or silent voice shouting agreement down her bones. She expected none, well knowing the difference between a symbol and the powers it stood for. Nonetheless, the answer to her question was plain.

She turned away and waved the cabin lights up, then went back to the desk, reached down for the comm control again. "Bridge,"

It was young antecenturion Khiy's voice. "Yes, *khre'Riov—?*"

She had to smile that so many of her people still called her that, though none of them belonged to the Service any longer, and the Service indeed would be the instrument of all their deaths were they ever caught. "The message which has just come in tells me what I thought it would," she said. "They are finally coming for us . . ." She could not hold back a somewhat feral smile. "We have much to do to prepare."

"*Khre'Riov—*" Khiy's voice held a most unaccustomed nervousness. "Are we going back with them?"

Ael laughed softly. "Did you truly think it?" she said. "Aye, going back . . . but never in the way they think, or the company. Is Aidoann still there?"

"Here, *llhei.*"

"Shortly I will have some more messages to send, and we must take care with the routing of some of

17

them, lest they come too soon where they are wanted. T'Hrienteh and I will confer about this at length. But first you should call the crew together. There are things to be discussed in detail before we go forward."

"Yes, *khre'Riov!*" Aidoann said, and the comm went dead.

Ael t'Rllaillieu gave the Sword in the Empty Chair one last glance, and smiled briefly; then waved her cabin door open, and went out to battle.

There would be those who said she had started this war. Ael was not so sure about that. *But beyond doubt,* she thought, *I shall be the one to finish it.* . . .

In the heart of Paris, just off to one side of the Palais de Chaillot, between the great reflecting pool and the Avenue Albert de Mun, stands the tall and handsome spire of the "troisième Empire" edifice built late in the twenty-second century to house the offices on Earth of the president of the United Federation of Planets. It was November now, though, and half the spire was hidden in the chilly fog which had come down all its lights. The mist had risen a hundred feet or so, but no more. Now the view from the terrace outside the room where the president was meeting privately with the chief of staff of Starfleet Command was mostly indistinct, with only a glimpse or two of distant buildings showing here and there as flitters and little ion-driven shuttles passed, and the mist swirled with their passing.

The room was very still, even though the door to the terrace was open, the mist muting the sounds of the city outside; and the thin pale light fell cheerlessly on the dark-paneled walls and the Shaashin, Kandinsky, and T'Kelan oils hanging there. In the middle of the room hovered a large oval sapphireglass desk on paired pressors, and behind it next to a matching cobalt-blue chair the president stood, his tall dark bearlike bulk slightly stooped as he looked down at the desk, reading from the display embedded in it. He had been up all night, and looked it.

"When did you receive the message, sir?" Fleet Admiral Mehkan said. He was a smaller man, considerably slenderer than the president, and very fair, as a lot of people from Centaurus are.

"It must have been about midnight," said the president, touching the display to bring the report up again. "The Strat-Tac people," he said, "are very thorough in their briefings. I'd thought this would have arrived a little sooner—but apparently her enemies back home have been making sure they have everything they need in place before they move."

"And now," said the chief of staff, "we have to start working out what to do . . ."

"Sit down, Dai, please," the president said. Mehkan sat down on a chair like the president's on the other side of the desk.

The president lowered himself into his own chair,

leaning on the desk while he finished rereading the report. "She'll have received the same message, I assume," he said.

"At about the same time, yes, sir. Her sources supply us as well, rather more directly."

"And you're sure that the source of the information is completely reliable."

"It's not just *a* source, Mr. President. It's *our* source."

The president nodded slowly. "I had wondered. . . . Well, the interesting part of all this," he said, "is going to be anticipating what she does."

"She has to have known they would come right after her," said the chief of staff.

The president nodded. "Unquestionably. If I understand the relative importance of the artifact she took with her, to produce the same result on Earth she would have had to have stolen the Articles of Federation, or the old Constitution, or the Magna Carta. . . ."

"Combined with the Crown Jewels, the Black Stone, and the Holy Grail," said Mehkan. "The Romulan government will do anything they have to, to get that thing back . . . or to make sure it doesn't fall into unfriendly hands."

"Such as ours," said the president.

Mehkan nodded.

"But it's still just an excuse," the president said. "They've been waiting for a chance like this for a long time. There are elements in the Senate which have been looking for a cause célèbre, something to push their relationship with the Federation out of the rut it's been stuck in for all these years. The Neutral Zone chafes them, limits their trading opportunities, annoys their expansionist and nationalist lobbies . . ."

"An excuse for them to push outward," said Fleet Admiral Mehkan, "would certainly be welcomed."

"Well, it's not as if there aren't also elements in Fleet which would welcome the resolution of a persistent tactical problem on one of our borders," the president said. "Massive resources are spent policing and patrolling the Neutral Zone every year. Everyone would find it an improvement if suddenly that necessity went away . . . wouldn't they?"

The Fleet Admiral twitched a little. The president noticed, and said nothing. "Yet at the same time," the president said, "no one has wanted the situation to resolve itself in an uncontrolled manner. Sometimes, unfortunately, you just don't have a choice. We've known for a while that there would be a war involving the Romulan Empire within the next five to ten years. Political tensions, economic pressures, even personal issues at high levels in the Empire have been bringing it closer and closer. Now here it comes: a little sooner than expected, maybe. But hardly unexpected."

He got up and came out from behind the desk, pausing in front of his terrace door and gazing out for a moment. Across the Seine, the lower half of the Eiffel Tower was now visible: the rest was lost in fog, producing an effect suggesting that someone had come along and sliced its top off with a knife. "That being the case . . . what matters is to protect our own people, naturally; but also to try to steer events so that they do the most people the most good over time, both on their side of the Neutral Zone and on ours."

"The altruistic approach . . ." said Fleet Admiral Mehkan.

"I know that tone of voice, Dai," said the president, beginning to pace slowly in front of that window. "I did Strat-Tac only a year after you did at the Academy, and I remember old Dickinson's lectures as well as you do. My job simply requires that I approach the problem from a slightly different angle. A wider one, maybe. War . . ." The president paused. "Any war is undesirable, Dai. A war that benefits one of your opponents at the expense of the other, and weakens both . . . that's also undesirable, but less so. However, a war that leaves you with, instead of two opponents who keep each other busy, only one opponent, now much stronger due to the defeat of the other . . . that is very undesirable indeed."

Mehkan said, "And things have been trending that way for some time, Mr. President."

"Yes. Well, events seem to be giving the forces in the Romulan Empire a different focus to 'crystallize out' around. We have two main concerns. Tactics, and readiness." He looked up at the chief of staff of

Starfleet. "And two questions. If we go to war with the Romulan Empire; can we defeat them?"

Fleet Admiral Mehkan was very slow to answer. "Strat-Tac says yes," he said. "But it would be a long, bloody exercise. There would be hundreds of millions of casualties, maybe billions, on both sides. And it would take both sides decades, if not a century or more, to completely recover."

"And if the Klingons come in on their side at the beginning?"

This time there was no pause in Mehkan's answer. He shook his head immediately. "A shorter exercise. A *much* higher death toll. The modern version of what they once called 'mutual assured destruction' . . . the possible loss of starflight capability to all three cultures, if things went on long enough."

"An unacceptable outcome, obviously. But I suspect Strat-Tac thinks the Klingons would wait to see how things went . . . then come in and attack the weaker of the two combatant parties at an opportune moment."

Mehkan nodded. "Their own Empire is slightly overstretched at the moment in terms of supply lines," he said, "and I think they're sensitive to the possibility that the Romulans, once hostilities were well enough under way, might attack the further-flung Klingon worlds with an eye to cutting off the trade routes to the inner planets."

The president leaned against the terrace door, gazing out. "Well," he said, "it's going to start. So our job is to keep this war from killing any more of us,

23

and any more of them, than is absolutely necessary; and to manage it in such a way that the powers left standing at the end of it are unlikely to go to war again for a long time."

"And if we can't?"

"We have to," said the president. "By whatever means. And one fairly straightforward means to the end is lying ready to our hand . . . if we use it intelligently."

Fleet Admiral Mehkan looked profoundly unhappy. "I wish we knew for sure that we could trust her," he said.

"We can trust her to be Romulan," said the president.

"That's what I'm afraid of."

"And we don't so much have to trust her," said the president, "as to anticipate her. In *that* regard . . . we have at least one resource who does that fairly well."

"I was afraid you were going to say that," said Mehkan. He got up and went to stand by the terrace door as well. "Mr. President . . . there are people high in Command who are going to resist this suggestion strenuously."

"You among them," said the president.

"Kirk is increasingly difficult to predict as time goes by. If he——"

"If we selected starship captains just for predictability," said the president, "most of them would be dead within the first year of their first five-year mission. Lateral thinking, creativity, the ability to outflank the dangers that face them . . . that, I would think, is the set of characteristics Fleet sorts for. Or have the criteria changed since we last did a review?"

"No, but—"

"You know what the problem is as well as I do," the president said. "It is not a question of predictability, in the case of the captain of the *Enterprise*; it is a question of loyalty . . . in this particular case."

"Only," said the chief of staff, "a question of where that loyalty lies."

"I have no doubts, in this case," said the president. "By the time things come to a head, neither will you. In the meantime, *Enterprise* herself has significant symbolic value to all sides involved in the argument which is about to break out . . . and that value would be much lessened with a change in her command."

He took one last look out the window, then turned back toward the desk. "So take care of it," said the president. "Get *Enterprise* out there. Cut Kirk orders that will protect Fleet if . . . action has to be taken." His face set grim. "But leave him the latitude he needs to get the job done. Our job, meantime, is to put together the assets she will need after the trouble starts. I want a meeting with the Chiefs of Services tomorrow at the latest. It'll take at least a few days, possibly as long as a week, for the Romulan force to materialize where we have to take official notice of them. We need to start putting our assets in place immediately, before it can possibly be seen as a

25

"Then we wait," said the chief of staff of Starfleet. And then . . ."

"The worst part," said the president, "as always. Get caught up on your sleep this week. *I* sure will, because once things start happening, we're both likely to lose plenty."

Fleet Admiral Mehkan nodded and headed toward the office door. Halfway through it, he paused and looked over his shoulder.

"There really *is* no way to avert this, is there," he said, very softly indeed.

The president shook his head. "This time, unfortunately," he said, "we're right. We're just going to have to pray we're not as right as we're afraid we are."

Mehkan went out. The president of the Federation let out a long breath and looked out the window again at the mist lying over the city, softening and obscuring everything in a veil of increasingly radiant obscurities as the sun now tried to come out above it all. The soft view would not last long. Soon enough would come the awful clarity of phaser fire in the darkness, ships bursting in vacuum, the screams of the committed and the innocent together. At times like this, he hated his job more than anything.

Nevertheless, he turned back to his desk and set about doing it.

On ch'Rihan, in the planetary capital city Ra'tlei-hfi, stands an old edifice built with the elegant classical proportions of the "Ehsadai" period—that time when the Rihannsu were new to their planets from the depths of space, and just beginning the business of taming the Two Worlds to their will. The building itself was much newer than the Ehsadai era, having actually been built after the fall of that terrible woman Vriha t'Rehu, the so-called Ruling Queen. The Rihannsu who built it were, like many of their people, looking back with both relief and longing to a time when the arts of peace and war in the Two Worlds had seemed to be at their height. By building again in that style, and incorporating what remained of the older structure on the same site, the architects hoped to remind Rihannsu everywhere of what they had so nearly lost to the tyrant—freedom, honor, the rule of ch'Rihan and ch'Havran by the millions descended from those who had crossed space to live there, as opposed to rule by the whim of any one Rihanha, however well-intentioned.

But memory is such a fleeting thing. Soon enough, within ten years, twenty, fifty, the tyrant's awful depredations were happily enough forgotten by people busy rebuilding their lives and countries after the wars that Vriha t'Rehu's ambition triggered. Soon enough, as the Senate and Praetorate resumed their ancient powers, the old jockeying for power began, as the few fought for influence among the many; and the people scattered across the worlds accepted this, once again, as part of the normal conduct of life . . . some few senators or praetors overawing their many co-gubernals by virtue of fam- ily connections or wealth rather than drawing them into agreement by common sense. The Rihannsu for- got, and the Senate and Praetorate were content not to remind them, that the Two Worlds are rarely in such danger as when only a few hold rule; and they forgot what the building meant, except that it was old and beautiful.

Now, on this morning of the thirty-fifth of Awhn, that building was still old; but its beauty was marred. There was a great crack running right across the massive low dome which was the central chamber's ceiling, roof, and another straight across and through the mighty slab of marble which had floored the great chamber under the dome, big enough to hold the whole Tricameron in session at once. Now for- mal sessions of both Senate and Praetorate were being held elsewhere while workmen labored among the ugly pillars and struts of emergency scaffolding inside the building; and outside, tractor beams and pressors were supplementing the normal stresses which had formerly held the dome unsupported over the chamber. The architects had planned superbly, but they had not anticipated that the Chamber would ever have a starship sitting on its roof.

The three men who stood there now, under the scaffolding, looked across the blaster-scarred and acid-stained marble of the Chamber and said noth- ing. The workmen, for the time being masters of this domain, paid no attention to them. The three men in their somber dark uniforms of state, sashed in black, not gold, were themselves paying little attention to the workmen. The gazes of all three were directed toward the far side of the room, where there sat an old, old chair. One of the workmen had thrown a couple ells' length of protective sheeting over it, but this did not disguise the fact that the chair was empty.

"Come on," said one of the men, the tallest of them, a big, fair, broad-shouldered man with a long, somber face. The three turned away and walked toward the entrance, which once had been perhaps the noblest part of the building, with its great bronze doors all cast and carved with episodes from the Empire's history. But the doors had sprung out of their sills when the ship came down, and were now off being repaired, leaving nothing but protective sheeting hanging down and crackling noisily in the hot fierce wind that ran down the streets of Ra'tleihfi in this season.

They stepped out into the day, a fair green day under that windy sky, and stood a little to one side at the top of the great flight of steps leading down into the city's central plaza, all surrounded and walled about with the close-packed spires and towers of the capital. A constant stream of workmen came and went past them, and also many city people, coming up the steps as far as they were allowed to see the damage done, and going away again, muttering. Tr'Anierh, the tallest of the three, looked at these casual observers coming and going, and said under his breath, "Perhaps we should seal this off."

"Why?" said the second man, the one in the middle; a short roundish man with a broad, cheerful face, bushy eyebrows, and hair beginning, perhaps prematurely, to be streaked with gray. "It's good for them to see what the damned traitress did. And what their taxes are going to have to pay to repair. Anything that brings *that* home to them is worthwhile."

Tr'Anierh looked over at the third of them—a Rihanha of medium height, medium build, medium skin tone, dark hair, a man almost resolutely ordinary-looking even to his customary bland expression—and wondered, as always, what he was thinking. "Well, Urellh?" he said. "Does Ahrm'n have the right of it here?"

Urellh tr'Maehlie let out a breath as if he grudged it. "It doesn't matter," he said. "It's not the people whose opinion will matter when we bring her back. It's the Senate, and the Praetorate. They're the ones who have to be reminded how she slighted them, denigrated their power, took the oldest symbol of it into her own thieving hands and ran off with it. When we go fetch her back, we must make sure that no distractions from outside keep them from killing her at last. More, though: we must make sure that they do not mistake her capture, and the Sword's return, as all that's necessary to bring this episode to an end."

"There's more to revenge, then," said Ahrm'n tr'Kiell, "than just her . . ."

Tr'Anierh looked back at where the doors should have been, glanced over toward the side-flight of steps leading out and down to the plaza, and moved slowly that way. The other two came with him.

"It's time we faced the realities," tr'Anierh said. "Things have been the same now for too long. We sit trapped here between two powerful enemies . . . one which has been kept from acting against us only by weakness caused by its empire being too far-flung for its forces to hold securely; the other by weakness at its root, a chronic unwillingness to fight unless forced to it by circumstances. And the first, as we now see, is shaking off its inactivity. The other is all too likely to do the same. Time we stopped acting the *hlai* trapped between two *hnoiyikar*, afraid to move one way or another lest one of the predators turn and bite its head off." *And ideally*, tr'Anierh thought, *time we found a way to get them to turn their attention to each other and leave us alone.*

"You sound," said tr'Kiell, "like the Senate yesterday."

"And the day before," said Urellh, "and the day before that, and for many days before. Endless cries of 'Revenge!' and 'Blood or honor'—but no one willing to lead the first ship out, against either side, for fear of being blamed for the bloodshed to follow." His voice had acquired an edge of disgust.

"And would you, then, Urellh?" said tr'Anierh,

31

trying to seem casual. But he turned away a little, not anxious to see Urellh see him holding his breath, or seeming in any way overinterested in the answer. *He has become entirely too sensitive to opposition, for whatever reason. If anything should make him realize how I detect his politics, everything I've been planning could be imperiled. . . .*

There was a long pause. "Aye, indeed I would," said Urellh. "The blow to our reputations, even eventually to our sovereignty, is a massive one. The insult grows harder to bear by the day. And others are watching. Not the Federation." His smile grew suddenly bitter here. "We see now what the Klingons think of a neighboring Empire which cannot stop one ship from coming in through our system defenses and taking the most sacred possession of our people."

"But that was treason. The defenses were taken down from the inside——"

"And what does that matter? The Klingons will say to themselves, 'Where once treachery's rank weed sprang up, it can be sown again.' No matter that it was chopped down once; they will see the ground as being favorable. They have always been willing to use such means if tactics required. And if treason does not work, they will use main force with joy. Any system which can be compromised by so few people, so quickly, has revealed a fatal flaw . . . and has revealed itself as easily broken by any who apply enough brute force to it."

"That flaw has been mended," said tr'Anierh. "Those people are dead now, or fled."

"Happy the dead," Urellh growled, "for they're beyond what will happen to those who fled, once we catch them." He looked over at Ahrm'n tr'Kiell.

Tr'Kiell shrugged. "If you expect news of new arrests, I have none. The Two Worlds are not a small place, and there are endless boltholes and empty places on both worlds where criminals and traitors can go to ground . . . especially on ch'Havran, which has never been as unified in its loyalties as it should have been. And then there are the client worlds . . ." He sighed. "Our intelligence services are doing what they can to find them, day by day . . . But it's a live traitor's nature to come out and take up his treason again when he thinks it will be safe. And those who helped the cursed t'Rllaillieu take the Sword will find that it will never be safe for them, no matter how long they wait."

"In any case," tr'Anierh said, "the matter is now, as you say, beyond choice. The Klingons have spotted what looks like a weakness at the very heart of our empire. They are already moving to exploit it. And it's when an enemy is moving that he is at his most vulnerable."

"We hardly have the forces to strike at them directly," said tr'Kiell, "with any hope of success."

"Not if we are the only combatant," said Urellh.

The others looked at him. "Communications are always subject to misunderstanding," Urellh said, "and misdirection. Even in peacetime: most cer-

33

tainly in wartime. And in the time just before a war, communications are more easily lost, misread or misconstrued than at any other time whatever. The Klingons are moving? The sooner, the better: for their movement will give the Federation pause. If word came to the Federation that the Klingons had struck—say, one of *their* outpost worlds—that news would serve to turn their attention away from us. With the result that we are left free to act—"

"They would not be so foolish as to become involved in a two-front war," tr'Kiell said. "It would be suicidal, even for them."

"They will become involved in whatever we present them with," said Urellh, "as always. They are not a proactive people, the Federation. Indeed, they are not a people at all, but a confused mass of hundreds of bizarre species with hundreds of agendas, all conflicting; they cannot act boldly or straightforwardly, by virtue of their very structure. It is a fact we have been slow to exploit. But now we will make up for some lost time, Elements willing; we will show them what a united people can do . . . and what real boldness looks like. Information, meanwhile, can be twisted into many strange and unusual shapes in transit between worlds. We will see what can be done in this regard in the very near future."

He fell silent, gazing out into the morning as some workmen moving slabs of white marble on hovercarries went by. Tr'Anierh was glad of the few moments' respite, for this unusually communicative mood of Urellh's had begun to cause him concern. *What trap does he set for us here?* tr'Anierh wondered. After a few moments, though, he put the thought away. The three of them, by virtue of long careful manipulation of the economic, dynastic, and political assets which chance and ancient House affiliations had cast in front of them, had over the past several years risen to the position of *aierh te'nuhwir*, "first among equals" in the Praetorate. Each of them, by virtue of sheer personal power, now swung behind him a considerable bloc of the votes in both Senate and Praetorate. Each of them knew too many of the others' secrets to be afraid of what the others might do. Tr'Anierh knew his fear, therefore, to be foolish: yet he knew the others had it too . . . and it kept them cautious.

"As for the Klingons," Urellh said after the workmen had passed, "they may come to see that the Federation is not invulnerable, either. There are members of their own legislature who would not be averse to sending their fleets in that direction, as much for the sake of changes in their own status quo as for revenge, battle, or booty."

"An interesting concept," said tr'Anierh. "But the main problem remains. The woman, and her cursed renegade confederates aboard our stolen cruiser *Bloodwing* . . . and the Sword."

He looked closely at tr'Kiell. "The Senate is ready to act," tr'Keill said. "If you think I have been acting to delay the matter, you think wrongly."

"But you have a personal connection," said Ure-llh, "and who could doubt that you would have mixed feelings about the situation?"

"I think the source of my mixed feelings is better dead," tr'Kiell said, "and enough said about that. With luck, the Elements being with us, it will soon be so." He fell silent for a moment, and then added, "And our other assets on *Bloodwing*, it would seem, are still in place; that confirmation was long in coming, and there was some uncertainty, but it came at last. So now we can give our increasingly noisy Senate something to do before it so completely loses its patience or its wits that it starts attempting to press the thorny chaplet of blame onto one of *our* heads." His smile was wintry. "They may safely be turned loose to enact the legislation which we will propose them tomorrow."

"Who did the wording?" Urellh said.

"I did," said tr'Anierh. "It needed some delicacy of shading. But the meaning will be clear enough even for the Senate, and our fellow Praetors will of course ratify it without discussion. The task force to be sent out on this foray will number six ships: more than enough both to handle the business of entering Federation space on a diplomatic mission, and to be able to pursue our own interests even if they attempt to block us. Most particular attention has been paid to the newer aspects of the ships' weaponry." He smiled slightly. This was his own area of expertise. "We will go to them, seemingly with our hands open, and demand the return of a war criminal for trial on her homeworld. If they turn her and the Sword over to us, that will be well. If they merely allow us to pursue her, that also will be well. She cannot long elude pursuit, and we will track her down and bring her and the Sword home—or just the Sword. And if they do *not* assist us by allowing pursuit, or turning her over to us——"

"Then war," tr'Kiell said.

"They will have forced us to it," said Urellh, in a tone meant to simulate regret. "We will have no choice but to do what is necessary to recover our property . . . and our honor. A evil chance, but some good will yet come of it. At best we will push them some ways back from the spaces they occupy on the other side of the Neutral Zone; there are some choice planets there. At worst we will do the Federation great and memorable damage along the border—destroying as many of the monitoring stations along the Zone as we can, and forcing them to spend vast sums restoring and restaffing them and installing new infrastructure."

"Hurting not only them," said tr'Kiell, "but various others who will realize that they have misperceived our weakness."

"Oh yes," said Urellh. "And meanwhile, in the first hours or days of that war, the first-in task force will locate the woman, whether she shelters behind the Federation's kilts or not, and destroy her and the Sword both, if need be. They shall not have her, or it; and she shall not live to keep it in our despite.

Better it should be destroyed than fall into alien hands . . . if indeed she is not more than half alien herself already, in heart. Likely enough, bearing in mind who bore her company at Levaeri V."

"And while we resolve the issue that started the war," said tr'Anierh, "the war itself will yield its own rewards. . . ."

"Perhaps more than anyone expects," Urellh said.

Tr'Kiell blinked. "I have little leisure to notice such things. If *ehlfa* should become a problem around my property, I would have the *hru'hfe* of my house call the exterminator."

"Ahrn'n, have you ever had an infestation of *ehlfa*?"

"Ah, but if you watched the exterminator, you would see something worth your while. He puts down bait and tempts the creatures to leave their nest. Out they march in their little columns. They find the prize. They tell each other the news with their body chemistry. Wholesale they race to the bait, falling upon it, busying themselves with worrying it into little pieces to take to their home. And while they do so, the exterminator comes to their home, all empty but for the king-*ehlfa* and his courtiers, and burns it. With their home destroyed, their king murdered, nowhere to go, the *ehlfa* are left distraught and witless; they wander away in every direction, and are eaten by predators, and the infestation is shortly merely a memory. . . ."

Urellh smiled. It was not a smile that tr'Anierh would have liked to have turned on him. "You are very bold," he said softly, "to speak of this under the open sky."

"In this company the news is safe," Urellh said. "But no other. After the way Sunseed was betrayed, and the DNA acquisition project with it, some harsh lessons about the need to know have been learned. Not least by me." He got a grim look.

"Can you actually be telling us," said tr'Kiell, "that the 'package' is ready?"

"Nearly," said Urellh.

It was this news that tr'Anierh had hoped against hope to hear . . . even though it also frightened him.

"So you are now suggesting," tr'Kiell said, "that we could seriously contemplate its delivery to one of the possible 'recipients' . . ."

"Or the other," Urellh said. "It is a matter of seeing which homeworld would be the most likely to endure such a 'delivery' with most of its assets intact. If the answer is similar in both cases . . . well, let both systems receive such a gift . . . But for now there is only one 'package.' The single prototype has not been tested: but testing it would reveal its provenance, and alert our enemies to a need to protect against it. So its first test must be its first use."

Tr'Anierh actually shivered, hoping that neither of the others saw. "So many billions of lives . . ." he said. "Even against *them* . . . even if it is only used against the Federation, Urellh, there will be questions among our own people. What do we say to them, afterward, when they come to us and ask us about the billions? . . ."

Urellh gave him a bland look. "A thousand dead," he said, "are a tragedy—a thousand million, merely a statistic. —And anyway . . . they are only aliens. What about our people, and *their* welfare? Think of how it could be for the Two Worlds and the client planets, to live in a universe where there was *no* Federation . . . *no* Klingon Empire . . . not anymore. No more striving to keep every ell of space or every Elements-forsaken dustbowl of a planet on which some few pitiful scraps of food can be grown. Freedom to be what we are, no longer fenced in, hemmed in, oppressed. Freedom to grow, to extend our boundaries and our culture right through the galaxy, taking what is ours to take . . ."

"Freedom," tr'Kiell said softly. "It is a noble dream."

"Freedom," said tr'Anierh, and for the moment said nothing else.

"What time does the Senate meet tomorrow?" said tr'Kiell.

"Eighth hour," said Urellh. "I will stand and propose the diplomatic mission at the ninth hour. All the important personnel are selected; all that remains is to have the Senate come to believe it has selected them, and then approve the assignment of ships in the usual way. They can be on their way by the threeday's end."

"Until tomorrow morning, then," said tr'Kiell, and saluted them both, and went on his way down the steps.

They watched him go, making his way down across the plaza and into the street leading to emn'Thaiven, the wide pale-paved Avenue of Processions. "There," said Urellh, "we shall lead the traitress to her death in chains, in not too long a time. And afterward we shall set about putting things right; mending the world, the Worlds, to be as they should have been long ago."

Tr'Anierh nodded, still saying nothing for the moment. The thought was in his mind: *What in the names of Fire and Air has come to this man, that he speaks so openly? As if he had nothing whatever to fear from anyone? . . .*

He glanced over to find Urellh looking at him: a casual look on the surface, but there was no missing the assessment in it. "I must go," Urellh said then. "Honor to the Empire, confederate."

"Honor," said tr'Anierh to Urellh's back, as he swung away and went down the steps in tr'Kiell's wake. Discreetly, from off to one side, Urellh's personal secretary came down along the steps to meet his master and began to speak to him, head down, as they went.

Eveh tr'Anierh watched them out of sight. He was filled with fear, but he dared not show it. *We are all riding the* daishelt *together now,* he thought. *No choice but to hang on tight to the horns, lest we slip back to where the claws can rend us. . . .*

He turned at last and went back up into the shattered building, to meet his own secretary and arrange

41

matters surrounding the speech in the Senate tomorrow. There were some other messages to be sent now, as well. Eveh started composing the first one as he passed through the clear sheets that hung where the bronze doors should have; and in that hot wind that ran down the streets between the tall graceful buildings of the Presidium, the sheets whispered together, saying *aish*, again and again, *aish*: the word for war. . . .

James T. Kirk finished rereading the report which had been appended to his most recent orders on the viewer in his quarters, and let out a long breath. For the better part of a month and a half now, he had been wondering, as he occasionally had before: *Where is Bloodwing?* . . . Now he thought the understood why she had made herself more than usually scarce. *But that's about to change.*

"It's happening," Jim said, "at last."

He looked up from the viewer in his quarters at McCoy and Spock. Spock was wearing that look of complete calm that only a Vulcan could assume; but Jim knew what was underneath it . . . or at least he had strong suspicions. McCoy was frowning, but then he had been frowning a lot since he came home from his last leave, a "vacation trip" which had wound up taking him a good deal further away from home than many people would have initially expected.

"The orders," Spock said, "are, on the surface, routine."

"As if any orders containing the words 'Romulan Neutral Zone' are routine," McCoy said. "Now or ever, but especially now."

"But the orders contain no such phrasing, Doctor," Spock said. "They refer only to the space around 15 Trianguli . . ."

"You know as well as I do, Mr. Spock, that any space in the direction of Triangulum and further away from Earth than about fifteen hundred light-years is hotter than the insides of a warp containment vessel," McCoy said, "and about as safe, at the moment. 15 Tri is plenty close enough to the Zone to provoke interest in some quarters."

"Those 'quarters' being the Senate and the Praetorate," Jim said, leaning back in his chair. "Who it seems, after the events of the last month and a half, are ready to start some serious shin-kicking."

He looked over at Spock with some concern. "The moment we start moving at all directly toward that space," he said, "word will get to the Romulans, either via moles in Starfleet or other intelligence sources here and there. And our movement will be taken as an excuse to start things rolling."

"Your analysis is likely to be correct, Captain," said Spock. "But the orders seem clear."

"Everything about them is clear except the time frame," Jim said. "They haven't come right out and told me 'Head in that direction but take your time about it,' but that's what the instruction factors down to. So I'll take the time." He thought for a moment.

"Scotty has been complaining about some adjustments he wants to make to the warp engines' matter-antimatter annihilation ratios: I intend to proceed at a leisurely enough pace to let him do that. At the same time, I know why they're sending us to the neighborhood of 15 Tri. We are intended to meet a ship, quietly, out in the system's fringes, to discuss a few things with its commander."

"And while we're doing that," McCoy said, "I have this feeling a few other ships may drop by to chat about this and that. All very informally, of course."

"Of course," Jim said. "But the Triangulum area being as lively as you say, Bones, I think we may dodge over in the direction of alpha Arietis first . . . bearing in mind that we may also still have a technological problem that we haven't yet figured out what to do with."

"Sunseed," Spock said, somber.

"The trouble with technology," McCoy muttered, "is that you can't stick it back in the damn bottle once it gets out."

"Any technology that allows a ship on the fly to create ion storms on demand," Jim said, "is too damn nasty to let out into the world. But here we are, stuck sitting on the thing. The Romulans would have used it as a weapon—*did* use it—which was bad enough. We took it from them lock, stock, and barrel, which was something of an accomplishment . . . but since we're certainly not going to use it, we need to find a way to make it unusable before it leaks out somehow . . . which it is eventually bound to, no matter how closely Fleet tries to guard it." He folded his arms. "Scotty has a few ideas on the subject, but he says he could use some assistance at the theoretical end. So we'll go get him some."

Jim looked at Spock. "Estimate of total time?"

"Four days and fourteen hours to alpha Arietis at warp six," Spock said, "from our present position. Then five days, twenty hours at the same speed to the neighborhood of 15 Trianguli."

Jim nodded. "See to it, Mr. Spock."

"Captain," Spock said, and went out. The door shut behind him.

McCoy paused. "There was," McCoy said, "something else."

Jim put his eyebrows up, trying to look surprised. "There was?"

"Jim," McCoy said, "this is no time to start trying to play the wide-eyed innocent with me. You should have started years ago, or not bothered at all. Now, I'm not going to ask for details about the sealed portion of these orders . . ."

Jim's mouth quirked into half a smile.

"But I wouldn't mind knowing," McCoy said, "whether I should start actively preparing myself to meet my Maker. Again."

"I'd have thought that after your little holiday on ch'Rihan," Jim said, "you'd be all caught up in that regard."

McCoy gave him a dry look. "And whether our

own side is as likely to wind up shooting at us as the other one. Or other *ones*."

There it was: the same concern that had been riding Jim for the past few hours, while he digested the content of the orders he'd received—both the parts that he could disclose to his crew, and the parts that he could not—and started to game out the way he thought things might go in the next month or so. "Bones," he said, "believe me, I'm going to be doing my best to keep matters straightforward. One side shooting at us at once is more than enough for me. But things can change fast sometimes . . . so you'd better fasten down anything that's loose in sickbay. And keep a chair ready for me when I need to come to talk."

"I'll take care of it," McCoy said, and went out.

The door hissed shut behind him. Jim sat down behind his desk and leaned back in the chair once more. He held that position for a good while, his eyes resting on nothing in particular. Then he reached out to the computer console on his desk.

"Computer."

"Working."

"Record a message and seal under my voiceprint."

"Recording."

"Latest communication received here confirms our last joint discussion on strategy. Meet us as previously arranged." He thought of signing it "Jim," but encryption was such a fragile and ephemeral art these days; the security of the message could not be absolutely guaranteed, and there was too much to lose should it be broken. Besides, he could just hear the laughter at the other end when the receiving party heard the signature.

"Code and send," Jim said.

"Working. Sent."

He hit the comm button again. "Bridge. Lieutenant Uhura."

"Uhura here, Captain."

"I just routed a message to your system. What's the subspace transit time?"

There was a moment's silence. "Judging from the relay address in that message's 'capsule,' I'd say fifteen hours."

"Thank you, Lieutenant. Mr. Sulu?"

"Yes, Captain?"

"Lay in a course to alpha Arietis, warp five, and execute immediately."

"Aye, sir."

"And Mr. Sulu—do you have a 'tank' session scheduled in Recreation this evening?"

Sulu chuckled, very low. "Yes, Captain. We're finishing up a round of tournament play."

"Maybe I'll stop by," Jim said. "Kirk out."

He switched his viewer to show the bridge screen's view as *Enterprise* made her change of course, a big wide swing to the galactic "southward," and added a warp factor or two, the blue-shifted stars pouring past her like so many burning arrows in the night.

I'd hoped I was wrong when I saw this coming, he thought. *But I was right.*

I just hope the trend holds. Otherwise . . .

He killed the external image and went back to studying his orders . . . looking for the loophole that would let them all survive.

Chapter Two

THEY CAME out of warp a scant light-week from Orundwiir, or alpha Arietis as the Federation stellar cartographers called it; a great blaze of a star, even at this distance, burning dazzlingly orange-golden in the long cold night. *Bloodwing* went sublight with all her weapons hot and her sensors stretched out to their utmost . . . and found no one there waiting for them.

Khiy looked up from his post at the steersman's console. "Should we decloak, *llhei?*"

"No, not yet," Ael said softly. "Let us wait our time."

Her people kept their eyes on their instruments, saying nothing for the moment, and Ael watched the screen, sitting in her hard straight command chair, and said nothing.

"They're late," said t'Hrienteh, in slight amusement. Ael looked over her shoulder at the ship's chief surgeon, who had been doing part-time duty on scan and comm for some time now while training the ship's last remaining junior officer in the position. "Possibly our time-ticks are out of synchronization," Ael said. "It would not surprise me; the computers have been through so much tinkering recently, and tr'Keirianh has not had time or leisure to look over all our shoulders and supervise as he would like to . . ."

"You mean constantly," t'Hrienteh said. "Fortunately, the Master Engineer must sleep sometimes." Her tone was wry. "But I very much doubt anything is really wrong with the computers, khre'Riov."

In reality Ael agreed with her. What she would not voice was her concern, even after so much evidence to the contrary, that something might yet go wrong with her dealings with the Federation, now that matters were becoming genuinely crucial.

Ael stretched herself a little in the command chair, gazing at the screen and admiring the giant midsequence star centered in it. Even away out here the brazen-golden fire of it was extraordinary, like Eisn but easily thirty times the Hearthstar's size. No one else was paying the great burning monster much mind, though. She glanced around her at the familiar faces, all bent to their work at the moment. There were different familiar faces on her bridge than had previously been here, for Bloodwing had lost about a third of her crew component during the operation at

Levaeri V, either in battle on the station itself or on *Enterprise* owing to her son's final treachery, and it would now be impossible to recruit replacements. *And will it indeed ever be possible?* Ael thought. For there would always be the chance that any new crewman picked up in passing would actually be an agent in the service of the Intelligence agencies based on ch'Rihan, intent on *Bloodwing's* destruction, perhaps even to the point of suicide. *No,* she thought, *for the time being we must just scrape along as best we can. . . .*

"Incoming vessel," t'Hrienteh said, and Ael glanced up. "Just dropped out of warp; subluminal now and decelerating fast."

"On screen—"

The view changed, losing that burning core. Instead, a faint golden spark reflecting Orundwiir's fierce orange light came coasting in toward them, the glow growing swiftly brighter as she came. Ael sat there and mused briefly over the numerous conflicting feelings that accompanied the sight of *Enterprise,* all gilt with the system primary's fire, approaching with her screens down, graceful, massive and—in these spaces—massively unconcerned. *How many times over all the years before Levaeri V did I wish much to see this sight,* she thought, *and to be lying nearby, cloaked, with weapons ready. And now the wish comes true. But how circumstances change with time, and how little satisfaction our wishes bring us once fulfilled! Yet another of the Ele-*

ments' small jokes with us . . . and if we are wise, we laugh.

"She is hailing us," Aidoann said.

Ael smiled slightly. It would not matter to Kirk that his ship's sensors showed nothing here while *Bloodwing* was cloaked. *He knows,* she thought. "Decloak and answer the hail," she said. "Barely two *stei* late, t'Hrienteh: I think you may forgive him that."

"Bloodwing, this is *Enterprise,*" said a familiar female voice. "Welcome to Hamal . . ."

"T'Rllailieu here," Ael said. "Thank you kindly, Lieutenant Uuhura."

"You're a shade early, Commander-General," said another familiar voice.

"Or you are late, Captain," she said, amused. "We have been discussing which might be the case. We really must see to it that our computers are better synchronized."

"Mr. Spock and Aidoann can sort that out between them, I'm sure," Kirk said. "Meanwhile, would you care to beam aboard? We have a lot to discuss . . . and when the first discussions are done, there are some people over here who want to greet you."

She watched *Enterprise* dump the last of her velocity and slip up alongside *Bloodwing* with easy precision, a very neighborly kilometer away. "I will be with you in a matter of some minutes, Captain," Ael said. "I have a thing or two to make secure here first."

She waved at t'Hrienteh to kill the communication, then stood up and stretched. "Your orders, *khre'Riov?*" Aidoann said.

"There's nothing needs done," Ael said. "Stand easy. But when did I ever obey any such request immediately, as if I had nothing better to do? Always wisest to leave even one's close associates a little uncertainty; a little room to wonder what one is up to. That way, if one day you must suddenly change your course, or your mind, without warning, you will have left yourself room to maneuver." She smiled.

"Even Captain Kiurrk?" Aidoann said, with a small smile of her own.

"Even the captain," Ael said, "may someday need to change his mind . . . or may have it changed for him. For that day, which may never come or which may be hard upon us, we must yet remain prepared. Khiy, the center seat is yours. Mind you match their movements exactly: their helmsman is watching you, and you know Mr. Sulu's sharp eye—you must do us proud. Come along, Aidoann, t'Hrienteh; we have a meeting. . . ."

Jim stood there in the transporter room in front of the console, which Scotty was presently manning. His hands were sweating.

Ridiculous, he thought. But at the same time, there were few guests aboard *Enterprise* about whom he had had more thoroughly mixed feelings than the one who was coming back aboard now. Here was a

53

woman who had sat in his center seat, and had some-how managed to look like she belonged there: a woman who had not only thrown him in his own brig—*well, yes, it wasn't as if I didn't cooperate—* but had decked him out as well—*all right, I returned the favor almost immediately, but still—*

He caught himself, and smiled. "Worthy oppo-nent" was the very least of the descriptions he might apply to Ael i-Mhiessan t'Rllaillieu; and there were others, more appropriate still, but he would not spend too much time thinking about them now. They would only make his hands sweat more.

He wiped them off against his pants and breathed out in brief annoyance. "Something holding them up over there?" he said.

Scotty shook his head. As he did, the door opened and Spock came in, closely followed by McCoy. It was just shutting when the communicator whistled. "Captain," said Uhura's voice out of the air, "we have an incoming shuttle."

Jim leaned over the transporter console and punched the comm button. "From the starbase?" he said. Starbase 18 circled Hamal's furious amber fire a couple of hundred million kilometers out.

"From the base, yes, but not Fleet registry," said Uhura. "ID shows the shuttle as registered off Hamal III."

"Aha," Jim said. "Very good. Clear the shuttle through into the bay: we'll be down to meet the pas-senger shortly."

"Yes, Captain. Bridge out."

The faint hum of the transporter came up. "Coming through now, sir," Scotty said.

Three faint pillars of sparkle began to form on the transporter platform; the light swirled, went solid, and the bodies it formed were held in a fractional second's immobility as they finished becoming real.

She was looking right at him, and Jim thought, almost with annoyance, *How does she do that . . . ?!* A little woman, slight, dark, slender, in the faintly red-glittering tunic of a Romulan officer, the sash across it glowing a subdued gold in the transporter room's low lighting; dark breeches and boots below, and above, long dark hair braided tight and coiled at the back of her head. She might have seemed unexceptional enough, except for those eyes—which even in this frozen moment held in them what seemed an uncomfortably assessing, knowing, look—and her carriage, even now like that something held proud and ready for a fight; a banner, a sword . . .

The shimmer of sound and light died away completely. "Commander," Jim said.

She glanced around her for a second, taking in her surroundings, and half glanced off to one side of her: then looked forward again. Jim swallowed. Big blond Aidoann t'Khialmnae, Ael's new second-in-command, was on the pad to Ael's right, as Jim had expected, and Surgeon t'Hrienteh, whom he remembered from the way he had kept finding her in McCoy's company when they were preparing the at-

55

tack on Levaeri V, was on the transporter pad behind her. But Ael's brief glance had been toward someone who was not there, and Jim thought of how he had first seen her son Tafv beside her, much taller than his mother, but as erect and proud. He would not now ever stand beside her again, of course; but it was poignant that Ael still carried herself, somehow, as if there were someone standing to her left, in his accustomed place. *If I have my own ghosts,* Jim thought, *so does she. . . .*

She came down from the transporter and reached out to take his hand.

He took it, not to bow over it, having learned that the gesture, polite enough for an honored lady on Earth, was charged with meaning for a Rihannsu which he didn't desire to invoke. He simply clasped it a little above the wrist, and she returned his grip and met his eyes forthrightly. The expression, as always, had an element of challenge to it, and more calm than Jim thought he would have felt under the circumstances.

She let him go. "Well met," she said, "so far into your own spaces, and after such a time."

"You're very welcome," Jim said, "in whatever time, and whatever space."

That elicited a shadow of a smile. "Commander," Spock said, stepping forward.

Did that assured expression become just slightly haunted as she looked at him? Hard to say; the look was concealed by the slight bow of her head to him, which Spock returned. "Mr. Spock," she said, "well met indeed." Then she straightened. "And Mr. Scott: do you do well?"

"As well as possible under the circumstances, Commander," Scotty said. Jim tried to keep his grin from getting out of hand. Scotty had been sympathetic enough to Ael, but her involvement with *Enterprise* had caused the ship considerable structural damage, some of it actually planned rather than as an accident in battle, and Jim suspected Scotty was already having misgivings about what kind of trouble her presence was likely to bring this time.

"As do we all . . . ," she said, possibly thinking along the same lines Jim was. She turned, then, and said, "Well, MakKhoi, and what of you?"

He simply smiled half a smile and reached out to squeeze her hand. "It can wait."

A few more moments were spent greeting t'Hrienteh and Aidoann; but finally Jim said, "The doctor's right, Commander: we shouldn't linger here. Someone else is arriving whom you should meet."

They all headed for the doors. "Someone from Starfleet?" Ael said.

"Occasionally," Jim said. "I believe her commission may have been reactivated for the time being; officially she's retired."

Ael raised her eyebrows. "I am sorry to trouble an elder's peace."

McCoy made an amused face. "Nothing much

troubles her," he said, "and, besides, this 'elder' is somewhere between one and three years old, depending on whose years you're using."

"Doctor," Spock said, "in Hamalki reckoning, it is considered an error of reckoning to separate out new 'incarnations' from the total life span——"

Ael looked over at Jim in some bemusement as they all got into the turbolift. "Doubtless this will be made clear to me shortly."

"As clear as it gets," Jim said.

There was some small talk in the lift, inquiries about Ael's crew and *Bloodwing*'s whereabouts over the past month or so.

Then the doors opened and they all stepped out. Jim was amused to see Ael's eyes widen a little at what they met first: a rugged rounded glittering shape nearly two meters tall and three meters broad, patched in what looked like rough amethyst, tourmaline, and ruby, with dark fringes all around that sparkled in the bright hangar bay lights as it moved.

Ael strode right up to that domed figure and stood there a moment with her arms akimbo, looking him up and down. "Mr. Naraht," she said, astounded, "what in Earth's name have you been doing to yourself to *grow* so great?"

The rough scraping sound that emerged was plainly a compromise intended for those who used airborne sound in its higher frequencies; but it was also plainly laughter. "Commander," said the Horta through his own translator, "just eating. But I'm told that's enough."

"We were a little surprised too, at first," Jim said, "but it turned out we'd been laboring under a misconception about sizes. The only full-grown Horta we had seen was the lieutenant's mother . . . and after many, many years standing guard duty over her eggs, she'd worn off a lot of her bulk."

"During the pre-hatching period," said McCoy, "it turns out the momma Horta doesn't have much of an appetite, and doesn't eat much. I suspect as much because she's a natural-born worrier as because of the basic biological setup of the species. But the youngsters have started coming up to the full 'normal' size for the species real quick, once they've passed latency."

"That is a relief," Ael said. "I would not have liked to think I had caused you to become obese by all that hyponeutronium I suggested you eat at Levaeri V . . ."

Naraht's fringes rippled. "It was a little uncomfortable for a while, madam," he said, "but I burned off the excess soon enough."

"Might have brought his growth spurt on a little sooner," said McCoy, "but that's all." He patted the lieutenant's outer "mantle" idly. "You want to slow down soon, though, son, or we'll have to keep you permanently in the hangar bay, and all you'll be good for is being dropped on people we don't like."

"I should say he has done well enough at that . . ." Ael said, with a wry smile.

"More than well enough," Kirk said. "Well, carry on, Lieutenant."

"Yes, sir. A pleasure to see you again, Commander," Naraht said, and rumbled away out of the hangar bay, filling the corridor outside nearly from wall to wall as he went.

They walked out into the hangar bay, where the ship which had just landed was cycling back into launch position on the turntable. It was of unusual design, an oblong four-meter-thick spindle of glassy ropes and angular shapes woven and melded into one another, some straight and edged, some smooth and curved, some even radiating into what looked like a brush of spines at what might have been the propulsion end. Even here under the artificial lights the "glass" seemed to keep something of the color of Hamal's sunlight, a gleam of dark gold under the glitter and sheen of the brilliantly polished surfaces.

The turntable stopped. As they watched, the whole smooth side of the craft facing them seemed to lose that smoothness, going matte, then revealing a fibrous structure like something woven or spun, then finally refining itself away to a delicate-looking webwork of threads that vanished away entirely, leaving what looked like a cocoon cut in half, all sheened inside with webs and points of light.

Down out of the cocoon stepped a glass spider—if spiders had twelve legs, each a meter long, arranged evenly around a rounded central body, the top of that body furred with spines of clear glass almost too fine to see, and a raised ridge of nubbly crystal running back to front amid the "fur," with four eyes in the middle of the ridge and two clusters of four eyes each, near each end of the ridge. With every movement of the much-articulated legs came a delicate chiming, and as the entity came walking, nearly waltzing, over to them, more chimes filled the air—a brisk staccato of glass bells, running up and down the scale, and saying, "What a pleasure to see you all; it's been too long—you're very welcome to Hamal!"

Jim stole a glance at Ael. She had shown surprise at the sight of Lieutenant Naraht before, but him she knew. In this case, she was managing herself more carefully—but Jim had seen this calm expression on Ael before, too, and knew what it concealed. "Commander," he said, "allow me to present K's't'lk. She's one of the senior Hamalki physicist-engineers associated with Starbase 18. K's't'lk, this is Commander-General Ael i-Mhiessan t'Rllail-lieu."

K's't'lk reached up one delicate limb and laid it in Ael's outstretched hand. "My great pleasure, Commander," K's't'lk said. "I've heard of your doings; and I hope to be of some service to you shortly." She cocked an eye up at Jim. "I hope you don't mind my bringing my own ship along, J'm."

"Seeing that we weren't going to be coming within transporter range of Eighteen," Jim said, "what was I going to make you do? Walk?"

She chimed unconcerned laughter at him, and Jim turned back to Ael. "K's't'lk and the *Enterprise* have had some history together," he said.

"Not so much history," K's't'lk said to Ael, "but a fair amount of mathematics. Though often enough, the two have come to nearly the same thing. . . ."

"When she's not rewriting the local laws of physics," Jim said, "she also does research in various areas of astrophysics . . . and one area which has been of particular interest to her has been the study and manipulation of stellar atmospheres."

"I see," Ael said. "That may indeed be of use to us all soon . . ."

"But what we need more first," Jim said, "is news. Let's take a break to get everyone settled . . . then we'll meet in the main briefing room and get caught up."

Hvirr tr'Asenth had thought he had known what cold was, before. Now he knew he was wrong.

Emni, behind him, was crying silently as they slowly walked. He would have dropped back to put his arm about her again as they walked, but twice now she had pushed him away, if gently enough, the second time whispering, "You already have Dis to carry; I can manage." And indeed she was carrying more than he was, at the moment, the few belongings the soldiers had let them take. But he knew the real reason that she would not bear his comfort. She was ashamed to need it. Hvirr could not see why: anyone would need it, in a situation like this. But there was no telling Emni that. She came of proud people, and was harsher to herself than anyone needed to be, especially now, when she felt she should be acting as Mother-of-House in their time of trouble, and a tower of strength. It was bitter to her that shock had derailed her strength, that she had gone along with all the others when the soldiers told her to, just like one more victim. *Maybe,* Hvirr thought unhappily, *it's just as well that she should find her pride a piece of baggage too heavy to take with her on this trip. Precious little any of us are likely to have left of it, by the end....*

The snow lay all around them, in drifts and hillocks blown among the tall narrow *maithe* trees, faintly reflecting what light of the stars in the hard black sky managed to make its way down through the forest's boughs. But the starlight was too little to make the going at all easy, and the moons were both dark tonight. For a mercy, the wind had died down, and the snow here was not crusted, but light enough to kick aside as one walked. But otherwise life, if this could be called any kind of life, went on for Hvirr and Emni and their fifty companions as it had for the last two days and a night: the endless marching through bitter weather, without a rest. Ahead of them went the faint light borne by the man who had volunteered to lead them, the one who knew the way over the pass. *And how sure are we of that?* Hvirr thought, desperate, trying to swallow, finding nothing to do it with: his mouth was dry as any desert. *What if he gets us lost? We will all die out here.*

Though I suppose it is preferable to being shot. It was supposedly a merciful death, the death by cold: weariness, then sleep, a sleep from which there was no waking—

Hvirr grimaced in anger, shook his head. Ice crystals cracked and fell away from his coat hood and neckwrap at the gesture. Hvirr gazed down sadly at the wrapped-up bundle he held, and hoped that the wrapping was enough. Dis was only two, and had always been somewhat delicate of health. Still, he was sleeping: that was better far than him being awake in this frightening dark place, so unlike the sunny little house in the valley, where they had lived until three days ago—

The house. Odd how clear everything about it seemed now, in memory: the particular hiss the front door had when it opened, the sun across the flagstones in the front hallway, the warm clear light in the kitchen when the hearthfire was going and Emni lit the table lamp to do her late work on the family finances on her small computer. *Who has our house now?* Hvirr thought, no longer having the energy to even be bitter about it, only resigned.

Emni came trudging up beside Hvirr, then, her face wiped as if she had not been crying. But he could see the telltale darkness in her cheeks, the chapping already starting from the cold. It was why Hvirr had stopped letting himself cry many hours ago, though desperately he wanted to: he had miseries enough already without adding chilblains to the list. "How is he?"

"Asleep, I think. Oh, I wish I were too."

He nodded, swallowing, finding it hard, with his throat so dry. "Don't think about it," Hvirr said, "it just makes it worse."

"I am so angry," Emni said, though the weary, dreamy tone of her voice made it seem a strange declaration. "And all our neighbors standing there, letting it happen. After all the years we've been there. Could none of them have said a word?"

"It's hard to find your voice sometimes," Hvirr said, "when the ones you'd try to convince are holding guns, and you have none." The memory of that first gun, on his own doorstep, was burned into his memory as if lightning had etched it there. A great misshapen ugly thing, eloquent of imminent death, with an emitter bell that seemed big enough to put his head into—it seemed to float there by itself, until Hvirr comprehended, in the clear bright light of the morning, that it had a man attached to it, that the man was wearing dark-green military armor, and that he was pointing the gun at Hvirr and saying, "You have ten minutes to get your stuff and get out." At first it had seemed like a joke, like a misunderstanding.

"Get out? Why, what's the matter?"

"Get out," the man said, bored. "Relocation order. All the people on this list—" He flashed a padd at

65

Hvirr, not even letting him look at it. "You're to be out of the town in an hour. Twenty *stai* away by noon tomorrow."

"But where will we go?"

The soldier had already turned his back on Hvirr, not leaving, but just dismissing Hvirr as something he didn't have to deal with anymore. Then Hvirr realized that what he and Emni had seen on the news was happening to others, on this continent of Mendaissa—the forced relocations that had seemed so unnecessary, so sad, so distant—were distant no longer. It was happening here, happening to them.

They had gathered together everything they could: some food, some spare clothes, their credit chips, Emni's little computer and the charger for it. One of the others who had been turned out, a distant neighbor whom they knew by sight, having seen him at market sometimes in the next town over, came to the little confused knot of them, maybe twenty people from six houses in Steilalvh village. Nothing's happening over there, it's safe. Come with me and we'll all get out of here together. Have you got warm clothes? Then hurry, come on—"

That was when this unreal walk had begun. Morning, through afternoon, through night, through the next morning, the next afternoon, and night again . . . It was twenty minutes in the co-op flyer, this journey to Memmesh town, over the pass. Never in Hvirr's wildest imaginings had it occurred to him that he might ever walk it. The pass was two *stai* up in the clouds, for Fire's sake! But now they had come over it, gasping for air—and filled with terror, for Dis had turned dark green as he slept—and all of them had survived, the child getting his proper color back quickly. That had been this morning. Under cover of the trees, though they had been walking for a day already, they kept going, hearing the constant scream of iondrivers and impulse engines overhead—the sky suddenly alive with cruisers and government shuttles. This too they had heard about the news: that the space around the Mendaissa and Ysail star systems was being fortified against possible Klingon invasion, that the government would protect its people—that to help it protect them, certain unreliable elements of the population were being removed from security-sensitive areas—

That was us, of course, Hvirr thought. *And everyone else in this part of the country who has Ship-Clan connections.* "It's the big spaceport at Davast," he had heard one of the people farther up the line mutter to someone else, her brother, Hvirr thought. "They're worried about security, there have been attacks on some other planets . . ." Her voice dropped to a whisper. Even among themselves, those who had been driven out of the valley didn't want to be caught talking about it. Even here, who knew, there might be spies. . . .

But they were on the downhill side now. It was, their guide had come back to tell them, earlier in this second darkness, only a few more hours. The path had been getting easier, even if the snow was no less deep. "I only wish I knew where we were going."

"Memmesh, dear one."

"I don't mean that. I mean afterwards. We can't stay there, they won't have room for all of us . . ." She looked at Dis, in Hvirr's arms. "He's been sleeping so much," Emni said. "I hope he's not sick." She paused.

"But then I suppose we should count ourselves lucky," she continued. "Other people had their money taken from them too, the soldiers charged them to let them get out of villages they'd been commanded to leave on pain of being shot." The bitterness briefly showed its edge in her voice again, then sheathed itself once more in weariness. "At least we've still got a little . . ."

Hvirr did not say that he wasn't sure it was going to do them any good. Anyone who had both Ship-Clan blood and a scrap of sense would try to get off the planet now. But there was no one who could take them, legally: and those who would do it illegally would charge the sun and both moons for passage.

"This is all my fault," Emni said. "Because I am Ship-Clan."

"Don't be a silly *hlai*," said Hvirr. "As if you could choose your heredity!"

He looked up, then, for ahead of them was a rustling, a shuffling; he could see the people up ahead bunching together, hear a kind of confused murmur from them. The path through the woods flattened out, there, opened up: he could see the green-blue of sky past and through the trees.

Hvirr scuffed through the snow toward them, craned his neck to see what they were looking at. Behind him Emmi came up and looked too.

Down there was Memmesh village. Landed around its scatter of houses, in the thin snow sifted over its surrounding pastures, were five or six government armored shuttles, shining their hot bright spotlights around in the dark. Another shuttle came screaming right over their heads as they stood there, heading down toward the village. Down there, tiny specks of men were standing around some of the houses, gesturing with tiny, tiny guns: and men and women and children were being driven out into the cold dark night.

All their group stood there silent. Hvirr heard someone say softly, "Where will we go now?"

And Dis woke up and began to cry.

It was not a meeting of all the ship's department heads: Jim would call for that later, when the circumstances into which they were moving were clearer to him. *And when they've become clearer to Starfleet,* he thought, hoping desperately that that hour would come soon. For the moment, all that was needed was a consultation among allies. That was likely to become thorny enough.

Ael seated herself down at one end of the table in the briefing room with her officers to either side of her; Jim took the other end of the table with Scotty

69

and McCoy, and Spock in the angle of the table at his usual spot handy to the computer. K's't'lk stood, that being more comfortable for her than any of the seating presently in the room. "T'l," Jim said as they all got settled, "I've sent for a proper rack for you: it'll be here later."

She laughed, a brief arpeggio of bell music. "It's no issue, J'm."

Everyone finished settling themselves, and Spock finished setting up the computer to minute the meeting. "Commander?" Jim said.

She bowed to him a little from the other end of the table. "Captain, before you spell out the details of why you have sent for me—not that I do not believe I already know—I would like to ask for your assistance. Or more specifically, Mr. Spock's."

"Anything, Ael."

She produced one of those wicked smiles which had once or twice before made Jim sorry to have offered her carte blanche. But it didn't last; he was being teased. "Mr. Spock," Ael said, "I would welcome some assistance with an assessment and reorganization of *Bloodwing*'s computer systems. We are shorthanded after Levaeri V, and have been forced to automate many more of our systems than we would normally prefer. Also, both the programming and hardware we have been forced to install for this purpose are very much of the improvised sort. If you would be able to assist us, I would be in your debt."

"Commander, it would be my pleasure," Spock said.

"Thank you, sir, Tr'Keirianh, my chief engineer, will confer with you." Ael looked back down at the table at Jim. "In the meantime, Captain . . . perhaps you will tell us what *you* know of the news I have heard."

Jim nodded and glanced around the table at the others. "The Federation has received a communication from the Senate," he said. "This came as something of a surprise . . . or rather, it was allowed to seem as if it came as something of a surprise. In any case, the Senate has asked permission to send a diplomatic mission across the Zone into the space in the Triangulum area: six ships. The Senate's message said they had something to discuss with the Federation which was too important to trust to the third-party means of official communication which are all that have been used officially for the years since the First Romulan War and the treaty which ended it. They were no more forthcoming than that, at first . . . but in the unofficial communications associated with the official one, there were some hints."

"It is, of course, me they want," Ael said. "I wonder, though, whether I should be insulted."

McCoy gave her a look. "Insulted? Why?"

"Only six ships, Doctor? They value me too lightly."

"It might begin with six ships, Commander," Spock said, "but it most certainly would not stop there."

"No," she said, "I know that, Mr. Spock: forgive my jesting."

71

"Mr. Spock is right," Jim said. "Where it will all stop is very much the question. Fleet has been treating the matter—not casually, of course; no feeler from such a formerly unresponsive source would ever be treated casually. But without any overt show of alarm."

"Nevertheless," Ael said, "I would imagine forces in the Federation quietly converging on Triangulum space and this side of the Arm."

"Not just Federation forces are moving," Jim said. "Your people are shifting ships around as well . . . even with our limited sources, and the only other source of hard information being the monitoring stations scattered up and down the Neutral Zone, we can tell that much. The Klingons are moving, too."

Ael nodded. "That I too had heard. I have become an excuse, then, for more than just my own people."

"I would say, though," Spock said, "an excuse that has long been sought. Am I correct?"

Ael's smile acquired a bitter edge. "It has been sought since well before *Enterprise* and *Bloodwing* visited Levaeri V together. The Rihannsu have been feeling confined and harassed for a long time . . . and now, with the Sunseed routines stolen and the mind-control project destroyed after nearly fifteen years of work, both panic and fury are running high; for once more the Praetorate and Senate feel their old enemies putting on the pressure. They will feel they must do something to defuse it. But they will not be satisfied with merely defusing it at home. Their least goal will be to take me back. But a better one will be to set you and the Klingons at one another's throats, while destabilizing the Neutral Zone as much as possible."

Ael looked very calm, but Jim knew quite well what turmoil her mind must be in. "Leading up to that goal, and after it . . ." Ael said. "There are many ways this business may go. But first I must ask you, Captain——"

"What Starfleet's intentions are toward you?"

Ael's regard was steady. Jim hoped his was too. "They haven't yet confided that information in me. I think they may not be sure yet which way to jump. I imagine we'll know within a few days. Meanwhile, *Enterprise* is one of the ships detailed to meet the diplomatic mission, most likely because Starfleet considers it to be a name that the Senate and Praetorate respect . . . and because they assume that where we are, you will feel secure in being also."

"When we eventually arrive at the scene," Ael said,, "yes; for I doubt Starfleet will want me sitting under their noses while the negotiations are ongoing. My people might be tempted to some improvident action." She gave Jim a mischievous look. "Meanwhile, I must tell you that whatever Fleet decides, I have no intention of allowing the diplomatic mission to take *Bloodwing* back with them."

"It might not be *Bloodwing* per se that they're after," McCoy said.

Ael favored him with a small dry smile. "At the end of bargaining, Doctor, perhaps not," she said. "But the bargaining will certainly begin with nothing

73

less. They will tell you they must have their property back, and the traitor crew that took it, and the woman who led them to do so, and the Sword she took with her when she left ch'Rihan last. As circumstances shift, they will allow one or another of the counters to be knocked off the table. Probably the ship first: then her crew. But they will by no means agree to settle for less than me and the Sword. And at the last, they will throw both of us away—kill me and destroy the Sword—rather than allow either of us to remain in your space or to escape their vengeance."

Spock had folded his hands together and steepled the fingers, and was looking at them in a contemplative way. Now he glanced up and said, "Commander, you have said what you will not allow to be done with *Bloodwing* and her crew. But you say nothing of what you have planned for the other two 'counters' on the table."

Her look was as controlled a one as Jim had ever seen from her. "Perhaps you would not be surprised," Ael said, "to know that I, too, have not yet made all my choices. My own options are still falling into place, and it would be premature to speak of them until I know more of where they lie." She sat straighter in the chair. "But I tell you now, I shall not go back with them willingly. Nor will I allow the Sword to go back. Flight would not be my choice, should worst befall; but I would consider it . . . except that it would help nothing. You would still be left with a war on your hands. For they will have war, now; never doubt it."

She folded her hands too, and stared at them.

"That's a certainty we will try to avert," Jim said, "and at the very least, we'll try to spoil their guesses on the way. If they get a war, it won't be the one they want."

"So long as it is not also the one we *don't* want," Ael said, "I am with you, Captain: so there let it rest awhile."

"We've still two issues which will need resolution pretty quickly," Mr. Scott said. "First, is there any chance they might resurrect the mind-control project which was housed at Levaeri?"

"The scientists originally involved in that project are nearly all deceased," Spock said, "and the research could not be reconstructed without both their notes and large amounts of Vulcan genetic and neural material. We are in possession of all the first; and, Vulcan now having been warned of the danger, they will never again be allowed to acquire the second. This reduces the threat to an extremely low level, in the short term."

"In any case," Jim said, "the main danger would be if Vulcans were going to be involved in this operation. But the word from Starfleet is that they will not."

"Possibly this is appropriate," Spock said. "For there are as many Vulcans who are sensitive about dealing with or admitting their relationship to Romulans as there would appear to be Rihannsu who prefer not to think too closely about Vulcans." He glanced over at Ael.

She bowed her head once in agreement. "Perhaps better that they should not be involved," she said, "for the sake of the ways the relationship may find room to change in the future."

She folded her hands and looked at them thoughtfully. "I should also mention," Ael said, "that while I was once able to acquire information about that particular clandestine operation through my connections to the Praetorate and my family's spies in the Senate and the government, my sources inside the Empire are now very few indeed. And while they suspect that there are more clandestine operations going on at the moment, it has proved impossible to get the slightest whiff of what they are. Alas, the government has learned its lesson after Levaeri. But it would be wise to assume that they are preparing some deadly stroke against you. You should sift all your present intelligence carefully for communications that seem to make little sense in context."

"The second problem," Scotty said, "is Sunseed."

He touched a control on the computer pad in front of him. The hologram projection field came alive over the table, suddenly full of the image of a star, its great sphere burning orange-gold. "The star's the one we seeded in the escape from Levaeri V," Scotty said. "I've used its data set, and as you asked, Captain, besides the ships that followed us, I've added a class-M planet at a distance from the star equivalent to what Earth's distance would be from Sol—"

Two tiny points of light came diving in out of the darkness that surrounded the star: two starships, *Enterprise* and *Intrepid*. The frequency of light in the hologram changed so that the color of the star's chromosphere dimmed down and the corona brightened into visibility, an even pearly shimmer, about half a diameter wide, surrounding the star. It was even, anyway, until the starships dove into the corona itself and began to swing close around the star. Their phasers lanced out in slim lines of light, and infinitesimally small bright sparks leapt out from them into the lower levels of the corona—photon torpedoes. "We were doing warp eleven at the time, so it's all much slowed down, of course," Scotty said, as the ships arced through the corona, now beginning to writhe and flare around them with horrible and unnatural energy.

The ships streaked away, out of the corona, out of view. The corona wreathed and threw out long warped streamers after them, almost like a live thing trying to catch its tormentors. The coronal streamers reached much farther out than seemed normal, on all sides now, attenuating, overextended, a rage of ionized plasma—

And then the corona simply collapsed back against the star, falling flat, vanishing. For a long horrible moment, nothing happened—

Flash! A blinding sphere of high-level ionization

77

leapt away from the star and blasted outward. The pursuing Romulan vessels that dove into view and toward the star a few moments later were caught by it. The effect, powerful enough in its first flush to propagate into subspace, deranged their warp fields. In tiny flashes of light they were annihilated, blown to plasma, and the plasma swept away before the relentlessly expanding front of an ion storm a hundred thousand times more powerful than anything that nature could have produced.

The view changed, backed off hundreds of millions of kilometers to show a planet like Earth—laced about with the orbits of satellites, patched under its swirls of creamy weather with the sapphire blue of seas, the greens and browns of continents, and on the nightside, great spills and spatters of the lights of civilization. Past that planet, its innocent-looking star was visible, but so was the only faintly visible wall of furious ionization that was tearing toward the world through local space. "I've sped it up a little now," Scotty said, "and marked it, for there'd be no seeing it this far out except with instruments. Ten minutes or so, this would take. But now—"

Like a tidal wave, completely invisible but marked as a hot blue line in the reconstruction, the ion storm struck the bowshock of the planet's magnetic field. For a fraction of a second, a faint glitter of massive particle annihilations and alpha and beta emissions manifested itself along the intersection's curvature, but the bowshock could offer no slightest resistance to an event of such intensity. The ion storm blasted past and through it, stripped away the planet's Van Allen belts, and a second later swept over the world in a wavefront now some forty thousand kilometers thick.

In orbit, every satellite was either scorched out of commission or simply slagged down to a lump by the sheer intensity of the radiation. A second later the whole planet's atmosphere was a maelstrom of hectic light from top to bottom. The upper reaches and the ozone layer went wild with blue and green and white auroral fire, not just the usual small circles one saw from space when a star hiccuped a minor flare at one of its satellite worlds, but huge interlocking circles that grew and ran across and around the planet's sphere, indicators of massive imbalances of potential. Millions upon millions of massive lightning strikes five or ten or twenty miles high leapt up from the ground or down to it everywhere; cities went dark as power grids went down all over that world, overloaded or destroyed; weather systems had imparted to them huge doses of heat energy that would derange the planet's entire atmospheric ecology with days or weeks of violent windstorms and vicious torrents of rain. Shortly there was no light left on the planet's surface but that of the scourge of lightning which would take days yet to die away, and the millions of wildfires the strikes were still kindling, while the upper atmosphere convulsed and rippled, burning blue with continuing ionization, and the tattered remainder of its ozone layer evaporated away. The seeded star's storm-wavefront passed, raveling on out into the system, vanishing from view. But in its wake, the surface of a class-M planet was swiftly becoming an image of Hell. . . .

Jim nodded at Scotty. Scotty looked uneasily at the burning image, and touched a control: it vanished.

"You'll understand why Starfleet is sitting tight on the details of those routines at the moment," Jim said. "But they're not so foolish as to think they're going to be able to do so forever. The secret will get out—if not from the Romulan side, from ours. Starfleet's desire is to find an 'antidote' or counter-measure which will make the Sunseed routines essentially useless, and to disseminate that information freely to every inhabited star system. They want to teach every vulnerable system a way to make both ships and planets effectively immune to the routine, able to stop it as soon as someone starts to use it."

Ael looked doubtful. "That will be a good trick," she said, "if you can find a way to bring it about. Do not forget, either, that my people have been using this tactic defensively against the Klingons, along our shared border, for some years. They may start using it offensively against you . . . and not just your shipping. Any defense you can produce against the Sunseed routines may in itself suffice to save many millions of lives."

K's't'lk had been chiming gently where she sat. "The problem's interesting," she said. "I think for the purpose of simpler implementation, we can leave the 'creative physics' of my people out of this solution; the less elegant but perhaps more robust 'hard physics' of realspace and subspace will suffice us, since the forces we're dealing with are fairly straightforward."

Jim had to put his eyebrows up at that. He suspected that someone in Fleet might have had a word with K's't'lk regarding the effects of creative physics on species less able to deal with the idea of rewriting the basic laws of the universe on demand. *Something to ask her later . . .*

"Sc'tty has described the basic induction routines to me," K's't'lk said, "and they really are rather simple. For an ion storm sufficiently violent to propagate into subspace and disrupt the warp fields of passing traffic—not even as violent as the one we just saw—you need a star of type K or better, at least one starship of a minimum 'significant' mass, doing at least warp eleven, phasers adequately pumped to very specific energy levels, and between five and ten photon torpedoes. All these requirements fortunately put the effect out of the reach of most users except for planetary powers and large fleet-running organizations such as Starfleet and the various interplanetary empires."

"So what we need," Scotty said, "is, first of all, a mobile form of protection, for ships. But then we'll also need a way for a planetary installation, or even something ship-based, to stop the effect once it gets started."

"And from a distance," K's't'lk said, "without having to go chasing after the ships initiating the effect; and without too time-consuming a setup, either." Her chiming died away to a faint glassy tinkling for a few moments as she thought. "Well, it might be moderately easy to protect individual ships by very carefully tuning their shields to match the average wave generation frequency of the ion storm in question. Mr. Spock?"

Spock looked thoughtful. "That would require very swift and complete initial and ongoing analysis of the oncoming wavefronts of the storm. Specialist routines would have to be written for the scanning hardware, to maximize data input and minimize processing time."

Scotty was rubbing his chin. "Aye. But you want to make sure there's no degradation of shield function. Our shields are useful, but they're not meant to do too many things at once. . . ."

"I agree," K's't'lk said. "As for the 'heavy,' non-mobile implementation of a defense . . ." She chimed softly to herself for a few moments, then trailed off. "It *will* be a good trick if we can do that," she said finally, "since what you're essentially doing with the high-energy 'seeding' of the star's upper atmosphere is turning its corona temporarily into something resembling a quadrillion-terawatt cyclotron. All that energy has to go *somewhere* once it builds up; and out, in the form of one or two big bursts of ionized radiation, is the easiest place. . . ."

"Well," Jim said, "I think we can safely leave the problem with you three for the moment: please get to work on it. Meanwhile, we have the matter of the incoming diplomatic mission to deal with. Another five Starfleet vessels will be meeting us at the preliminary rendezvous point, which is 15 Trianguli. We will then proceed to a spot not far from the borders of the Neutral Zone, and meet the diplomatic mission there. And then . . ."

"Then no one has the slightest idea what'll happen," McCoy said.

"Our only consolation," Jim said, "is that matters will take a while to unfold, and we'll have time to anticipate them. The negotiating team assembling on the Federation side apparently has instructions to attempt to solve some other outstanding issues as well."

"And will the Rihannsu embassy be empowered to deal with these as well?" K's't'lk said.

"We're not sure," Jim said. "This may prolong the proceedings somewhat. . . ."

"Possibly," Spock said, "that is a goal of the Federation negotiators . . . though one they doubtless would be unwilling to advertise more openly."

"I'd agree with you there, Mr. Spock," Jim said. "We'll depart Hamal this time tomorrow, to meet the other Starfleet vessels at 15 Tri in five days' time. Spock, will this give you enough time to have a look at *Bloodwing*'s computer installation?"

"More than ample time, Captain. I will start as

soon as we are finished here, with the commander's permission."

"Granted, Mr. Spock, most willingly." She bowed to him where she sat: then straightened and looked down the table at Jim. "Meanwhile, Captain, who is this who wishes to greet us?"

"About half the crew," Jim said, "as if you don't know."

"It will be my pleasure," Ael said, and rose; the others rose with her. She caught the glance Jim threw her, and said, "Aidoann, I will speak with the captain alone for a moment. Do you go with Mr. Spock and the doctor and the others: I will follow shortly."

"Yes, madam," said Aidoann, and along with Spock and McCoy and the others, she and the surgeon went out.

The door shut, and Jim looked over at Ael and said nothing for some seconds.

"It is difficult . . ." she said.

She has a talent for understatement, Jim thought, *but she always did. . . .* "Ael!" he said, "first, I wanted to thank you. For McCoy."

She shook her head. "But you sent me a message saying as much long ago."

"It could use saying again," Jim said. "Fleet sometimes sends us into very uncomfortable situations . . . and that particular one would have gone beyond discomfort and into the 'terminal' for Bones, had you not come through."

Ael raised her eyebrows. *"Mnhei'sahe,"* she said,

"takes forms that surprise us all, sometimes. But MakKhoi commands loyalties of his own, as you know. It is not an intervention I regret . . . mostly."

The smile flashed out just briefly, then. Jim grinned back. " 'Mostly'?"

"I have no regret at all for plucking him out of the middle of the Senate," she said, pushing her chair back and coming around the table to stand by him, near the window; they looked out at the stars together. "But I brought something else away with me as well. And *that* action . . ." She shook her head.

"It's a little late now for regrets," Jim said. "And if that hadn't happened as trigger, something else would have, eventually."

"I would like to come to believe you," Ael said. "That may take a while. But no matter. Tell me now why you were so little eager for our ships to meet where Starfleet initially desired them to, at 15 Trianguli?"

He had been afraid she would ask him that. "Mr. Spock," he said, "has given me some odd looks over that. A hunch?"

"Are you asking me or telling me?" Ael said, looking bemused.

"Neither," Jim said. "I simply didn't care for *Bloodwing* to be openly advertising her unescorted whereabouts at the moment . . . even indirectly."

"And that would also be why you desire to go no further in-system."

"Yes. It's a shame, because the starbase here is an

extraordinary piece of engineering and you would enjoy seeing it—the Hamalki are tremendous builders. But there are too many beings in-system who notice who goes and comes. Even out here, where there's a lot less notice taken than you'd get closer in to Hamal."

Ael nodded. "Starfleet, though, may be confused by the roundabout manner in which you are proceeding."

"Right now they won't mind a little confusion," Jim said. "They gave me some latitude; I'm using it. Later I may not have so much."

"And what will you do then?" Ael said. "When they order you to fetch me and the Sword back to where the diplomatic mission is waiting, and hand us over to them?"

He looked at her in silence. Then he said, "Maybe it won't come to that."

The look she threw him was ironic, and skeptical, in the extreme.

Chapter Three

IN THE normal course of things it was not unheard of, but it was unusual enough, for a single senator to be asked to meet privately with one of the Praetorate. When such a thing happened, the senator in question tended to attract a great deal of attention for days, perhaps months, afterward, as other senators and various lesser political figures, more on the margins of things, tried to work out which party had what advantage over the other. This being the case, Arrhae i-Khellian t'Llhweiir, the newest and least senior senator in the Tricameron, could well understand at least one reason why the summons to meet with the Praetor Eveh tr'Anierh might have come to her house so late at night: late enough for almost all the household to have long since sought their couches. What was still a matter of some concern to her was why she should have received such a summons at all . . . and how it might now affect her other business.

The whole place had immediately gone into a flutter. Those of the servants who were still awake woke half the others, for they understood the unusual nature of such a summons. Now half of them were terrified, and half of them were excited, and once again Arrhae resolved to get the secure comm terminal moved into her bedroom so that the whole place would not be disrupted every time an official call came through. When the terminal had first been installed a month or so ago, she had thought it was unlikely to go off much, and had had the workmen put it on a stand out in the House's Great Hall. But the wretched thing went off constantly, five or six times a day, and the shriek that the Hall's bright acoustics made of its alert tone was becoming a trial to her temper.

It had been worse for H'daen tr'Khellian, the Old Lord of the House. Every time the device went off he had resurrected some new and more awful language from his ancient days in Fleet, until Arrhae found herself half wishing it would go off, on some of those long hot late-summer afternoons, merely for the diversion of hearing him curse it. But finally H'daen had decided that this season in i'Ramnau city was too hot for him; and (since the House's fortunes had looked up somewhat with Arrhae's accession to the Senate) he had taken himself off up northward to the Edrunra Mountains northward, where the House had an old *ehto*, or summer shiel-ing-cottage. There he was busying himself bossing around the workmen who were renovating the place, enjoying the cool weather under the conifers on the mountainside, and reveling in the complete lack of comm calls of any kind whatsoever. "You want me," the old gray-haired man had said, on the morning a tenday ago when he took himself away, "send a flit-ter, Senator."

Arrhae had found no need for that. She was busy enough, and all too many of her afternoons were spent answering the wretched terminal, so that she would have had to leave her other business until late at night even if that were not her preferred time to handle such. Arrhae was not only a new senator, but was seen by some of her fellow legislators, she now realized, as a potential marriage-match as well. This amused her, for she was determined to remain matchless indefinitely, if not indeed permanently. She was frankly enjoying the experience of being an "independent," wooed and sought after by every fac-tion in the Senate, and she had no intention of doing anything except hold all her wooers, political and personal, at arm's length while she spent the foresee-able future assessing the situation into which she had newly fallen. *Besides . . . marriage would inter-fere with "other business." No, that would not be something to think at all seriously about.*

Meanwhile Arrhae knew that half the people who

called her, or called on her, were simply fascinated by the concept of a senator who, a month and a half before, had been a servant—*hru'hfe* of House Khellian, yes, the chief steward of the house over its other servants, but hardly anyone to be reckoned with. But one day it had all changed, as an Intelligence officer turned up on the House's doorstep with a Federation Starfleet officer in tow. Within what seemed no more than a matter of days, Arrhae had been threatened and intimidated by various Rihannsu, utterly terrified by a human, and then run over, under the very dome of the Senate chamber, by a Horta. A scant half tenday later than that, she had been brought under the poor cracked dome again and given her signet. It had been a very full month.

And now everything was shifting again. Arrhae stood outside the front gates of the House, with little old Mahan, the ancient door-opener of the House, standing behind her. *"Hru'hfe,"* he said, "you be careful now."

Arrhae smiled, looking up into the dark and turning the senatorial signet around and around on her finger, a habit she hoped she would be able to break eventually. He was ancient, was Mahan, and odds were good that he would never stop calling her that, no matter how other matters changed. For him there was only one lord of the house, the Old Lord, and a senator more or less under the same roof made no difference. "I will," Arrhae said, hearing the thin whine of a flitter coming through the darkness. "You lock up when I'm gone, Mahan, and take yourself back to couch. I may not be coming back tonight."

"When, then?"

The whine of the flitter got louder; she could see its lights, now, as it homed in on the landing patch in front of the house. "Possibly in the morning," Arrhae said. "Either way, I'll call and let you know."

"What if that thing goes off?"

"Ignore it," Arrhae said, more loudly, as the flitter settled before them, and its underlights came up more brightly to illuminate her way; its hatch popped, and a uniformed figure scrambled out of the seat next to the pilot. "Go on, Mahan! Sleep well."

But he would not move, and finally Arrhae walked away from him to where the officer stood waiting. He bowed to her, and said, *"Deihu,* if you would, kindly be pleased to enter the conveyance——"

It was a courtesy, but still Arrhae wondered what he would say or do if she refused. One did not usually refuse a praetorial request, even at one removed; such were assumed (by the prudent) to have the force of an order. Not that Arrhae would have refused this one: her curiosity was aroused. *And so will everyone else's be,* she thought as she gave the officer a fraction of a gracious bow and followed him to the flitter, *when word gets out.* It was half a string of cash to twenty that someone in the house was on the normal comm channel this moment, calling one of the local-world news services to tell them about this midnight meeting. Or one of the

Havrannsu ones: they were always slightly hungrier for news, for political reasons with which she was becoming all too familiar.

Arrhae stepped up into the flitter's passenger compartment. It was luxurious, but she was becoming used to this, though (she hoped) not too used to it. "Madam," said the young officer, plainly trying not to stare at her, and not doing too well at it, "there is a light collation laid on in the side cupboard. Also ale and wine, in the top one . . ."

"Thank you, *eriu*," Arrhae said. "I'm sure I will be perfectly comfortable."

"We will be in Ra'tleihfi in three-quarters of a standard hour, madam. If there's anything you desire——"

"Getting there might be nice," Arrhae said, she hoped not too tardly: but at the same time she was not a night person, and declined to pretend to be. The young man gulped and gently shut the door.

They lifted off lightly enough, but the flitter then rocketed forward at such speed that Arrhae was hard put to restrain her smile. *I must learn not to scold,* she thought. But for so long that had been a significant part of her job here . . . besides keeping her ears and eyes open, of course, on other accounts. The difference was that if a *hru'hfe* scolded, no one suffered from it but the household's servants. If a senator scolded, effects tended to be much more widespread.

And if a praetor scolds? . . .

One would expect serious trouble indeed. And this

was not just any praetor she was going to see, not merely some one of the Twelve. Eveh tr'Anierh was what, in the language she had recently begun practicing to think in again after a brief hiatus, would have been called a triumvirate. Except that triumvirs in the original context had been directly elected by the citizenry—poor, rigged examples of democracy though those ancient elections had been. These three men had acquired their de-facto position by means of manipulation of the other nine praetors, and to a lesser extent by favors done for the various power blocs in both houses of the Senate—as many for those who expunged laws as for those who enacted them.

And what in the names of Air and Earth does such a man want with me?

There was, of course, always that one fear, the one that would never quite go away . . . but probably safer that it did not. The only time in Rihannsu politics that people stopped asking questions about you, normally, was when you were dead . . . and sometimes not even then: for the actions of the dead could be, and sometimes were, used to incriminate the living. Arrhae, for her own part, was both alive and, if anyone ever got wind of what her other business was, exquisitely incriminable. Even now, in her present position—honored as a hero, elevated to the Tricameron, desired as a possible strategic Housematch—there was always the question: *What if someone has found out? What if he has found out?* All the rest of it would matter not a straw's worth in the wind, if that ever happened. Honors bestowed could be stripped away again . . . and the revenge on the party who had allowed them to be fraudulently bestowed would be most prolonged and painful.

Arrhae let out a long breath and stretched her limbs, then opened the bottom cabinet. *Dear Elements,* she thought, *do they fear I will starve in three-quarters of an hour?* The "light collation" looked as if someone had pillaged the Ruling Queen's cold table. *Look at all this!* Kheia, *roast* lhul, *sliced cold irriuf mousse,* ahhel *jelly.* It was just as well she had eaten lightly before bed: otherwise the sight of all this food could have left her feeling queasy. Still, she reached up for a cup from the top cupboard and poured herself a tot of ale, and then picked up a pair of tongs and smiled slightly. House Khellian was doing better than it had done in a while, but not so well as to afford *kheia* on a regular basis.

Quite shortly, it seemed, they were landing; either the pilot had made better speed than originally intended, or Arrhae had been paying more attention to the *kheia* than she realized. She put the eating things away and dusted the crumbs off, making a note to have the House's new *hru'hfe* inquire about the recipe. Then she peered out at the compound into which the flitter was settling, out of the glare of the roads and towers of Ra'tleihfi. Paths to and from the landing patch were lit, but the house at the center of it was not; that was a low long dark bulk, only faintly visible by light reflected from other sources, and in all of it Arrhae could see only one light lit in a first-floor window.

The flitter grounded most gently, and the young officer was at the door again for her when it opened, and handed her down. Outside, on the flitter patch, she found a small honor guard awaiting her. *In the middle of the night? Arrhae thought. For me, or is someone else more important here?* They raised their weapons across their chests in salute, and she bowed to them, another fractional superior-to-inferior bow, another of the things she was having to get used to these days—for a senator was almost everyone's superior. There were, however, exceptions.

"This way, if you please, *Deihu,*" said the foremost officer in the honor guard; and he turned. Arrhae followed him as he led the way, and the rest of the guard fell in behind.

They made their way toward the darkened house through the soft summer night. It was not a very old building, perhaps no more than a few hundred years in existence; and as they drew closer to the pillared portico that hid the main doors, the pale beige stone house showed no outward sign of the status of its occupant, which was still something that could happen even in these symbol-conscious days. But there was no missing, on the security vehicles parked outside, and on the side of the one that had brought her here, the taloned, winged sigil that gripped the Two Worlds one in each claw, and the characters scribed around it: *Fvillhaih Ellanna-*

hel t'Rihannsu, Praetorate of the Romulan Star Empire. If the Twelve themselves sometimes disdained making a show of their power, those who served them usually did not.

The officer commanding the honor guard went up a low flight of steps into the portico. Arrhae followed, and as she came up the steps, the two great doors in the shadows opened outward, to reveal a single tall figure standing there against the light. He was fair; that by itself was a little unusual for her adopted people, but just as unusual was his height, which would have marked him out regardless of his hair. He was dressed casually, but richly, in long kilts and a long tunic, appropriate enough for the time of night, but dark enough that he might have come from some formal engagement earlier in the evening and not bothered to change.

He stepped forward to greet her as she came up to the top of the steps. *"Deihu* t'Llhweiir," said tr'Anierh, "you are very welcome to my house, and at such an hour."

His bow to her was deeper than it needed to be. She returned the compliment, giving him a breath's more time than he was strictly entitled to. "The *Fvillha* honors me by asking for a consultation," Arrhae said.

"The *Deihu* is being politer to the *Fvillha* than necessary, given the hour," said the praetor, "and probably wonders what in the Elements' Names causes the praetor to call the senator out so late."

The man's wry look was open, and invited sympathy. Arrhae simply smiled at him: she was not going to discuss business out here.

"Dismissed," tr'Anierh said to the guard. They bowed, all, and took themselves away into the silent darkness.

"Please come in," tr'Anierh said. Arrhae followed him through into the light, and behind them the House's door-opener shut the great doors and went back into his little room. The hallway through which the praetor led Arrhae was nearly as wide as House Khellian's whole Great Hall, all done in polished viridian stone and dimly lit with only the occasional faint star of lamplight as suited the time of night; shadows moved under the high ceilings with the lamplights' flickering.

"It's a great barn of a place," said tr'Anierh as they walked. "Wonderful for entertaining, but a nuisance to heat in the winters. Fortunately I needn't pay the fuel bills: it would be my whole salary. . . . Here's my study, Senator: do come in."

A door slipped open as they approached one wall. This was the room Arrhae had seen from the flitter, with its light on. Here there was a wide worktable of polished blackwood under the window, and another, smaller, in the middle of the room, with two big black chairs drawn up to it and facing one another across the table, all on a carpet of a beautiful dark blood-green, very thick and soft to walk on. The walls of the room were all lined with blackwood shelves stacked with tapes and books and solids,

97

some of the stacks tidy, some of them looking about to collapse.

"Please, *Deihu*, sit and be comfortable," tr'Anierh said, going around to the chair on the other side of the table. "May I give you some draft?"

The polished clay pitcher on the tray down at one end of the table was plain reedgrain draft, Arrhae could tell by the scent, and frankly at such an hour she welcomed the prospect; the stimulant content would certainly do her no harm. "Please do."

"Spice?"

"No, I thank you: blue, please."

He poured, handed her the tall stemmed cup. Arrhae pledged him, drank, and took a moment to look at the table. It was not plain blackwood, as might have seemed the case on first glance, but was inlaid right around its perimeter with one long sentence in dark *heimnhu* wire. She traced the middle of the passage with one finger. "T'Liemha's *Song of the Sun*," she said. "What a lovely piece of work. . . ."

"They told me you were a cultured woman," tr'Anierh said, "and I see they were right."

Arrhae simply smiled slightly at this. Some of her new senatorial confederates had, on meeting her, made remarks to her of this sort. They varied between gracious and subtle to extremely silly, and mostly they factored down to meaning *I'm surprised you haven't come to Senate carrying a mop.* She raised her eyes from the exquisitely inlaid wood, and met his look. "I will not start polishing it, Praetor," Arrhae said, "if that was your concern."

His eyes widened slightly. Then he grinned at her. "Well enough," said tr'Anierh; "doubtless I deserved that."

She lifted the cup to him and drank again. "How can I assist you, Praetor?" she said. "It is surely late for both of us."

"It is that," he said, and rubbed his face briefly before picking up his own cup and drinking. When he put it down again, tr'Anierh looked slightly more composed. "Senator," he said, "you will have heard just now of the mission which the Tricameron sends to the Federation."

She would have had to be deaf not to have heard of it; the racket in the session yesterday had been extraordinary. "Indeed so," Arrhae said. "A most historic time is upon us."

"Yes," tr'Anierh said. "And we have ... some concerns."

She gave him a questioning look as she drank. "That would be understandable," she said. "But about what, exactly?"

"Do you know the names of the party who are going?"

"A great list of them was read out in session," Arrhae said, "which the Senate approved by acclamation. I confess I only recognized about twenty of them; but things were happening rather quickly then."

99

"The names of the chief negotiators, though, you may have recognized."

"Oh yes," she said. Several of the names had figured prominently in the trial of a Federation Starfleet officer here recently, all people who had been profoundly annoyed at having been cheated of the sight of his execution. Others Arrhae knew as jurists, or senators of considerable seniority; if they shared one characteristic that she knew of, it was a near-hysterical hatred of the Federation. When the senators in question spoke on the subject in session, they did not so much speak as froth at the mouth.

"How do you like of them?"

Arrhae started to have a suspicion where this was leading. She wondered how most safely to proceed.

"They are very . . . emphatic," she said, "in their opinions."

Tr'Anierh gave her another of those wry looks.

"So they are," he said. "I would like to add a name to the list of those who will go." He let the remark hang in the air until she grasped its meaning.

"*My* name?" Arrhae said. "*Fvillha*, I beg pardon: but why me?"

He sat back in his chair. "For one thing," he said, "you are an independent; and genuinely so, for you have had no time to be coopted—not that I think that would come soon, anyway: even your casual conversations have already made your stance fairly plain." Once again Arrhae drank, meanwhile reminding herself never to forget how closely she was listened to.

"Nearly every other member of the party which will go with this mission is already chained down tight to one or another of the five great blocs. It would, I think, be in the Praetorate's interest to see that there are at least a few senators on hand whose perceptions of our enemies, and whose reactions to what they may say, have not already been dictated by someone else."

Arrhae nodded. "But you have another thought as well."

"You have had dealings with humans recently," tr'Anierh said.

It was hard not to freeze. Arrhae put her cup down on the tray, and said, "It is not an easy business at the best of times."

"I think you may be in a position to understand them better than many of us might," said tr'Anierh. "And that position might enable you to perceive something, or discover something, about the Federation negotiating position, or their situation, which others of us might miss . . . and which might make a very great difference to the Empire in the long run."

The only thing Arrhae could do was laugh. "Praetor," she said, "a few conversations in a storeroom are all the experience I can bring to this exercise. You honor me very greatly, but I think maybe it would be a skilled translator you would find best fitted to this work."

He gave her a thoughtful look. "If there are personal reasons you would not choose to travel at this time—"

"Not at all," Arrhae said. "But I am very uncertain how much good I could do. I would serve gladly, but—"

"But will you go?"

There was something odd about his intensity. Arrhae did not know what to make of it. It came to her, then: *I must go. I must find out what is behind this. And I certainly will not find out if I stay here.*

"*Fvillha*, I will go," Arrhae said, "and I will try to do my Empire honor."

"Senator, I think you cannot fail to do so," tr'Anierh said. "The mission will be leaving tomorrow evening. Can you be ready by then?"

There would have been a thousand things to do first if she were just a *hru'hfe*: but if she were, she would hardly be being asked to go on a diplomatic mission. Some formal clothes would be what she needed to pack; not a great deal more. "*Fvillha*, I can."

"That is good news," tr'Anierh said. "I will arrange for you to be billeted aboard *Gorget*, where the most senior members of the mission will also be. There are people attached to the mission, administrative staff and so forth, who will make themselves known to you over the first couple of days in warp; they will have leisure to explain to you the kind of concerns we have at the moment about the conduct of the mission . . . and I would urge you to do all you can to help them. Other details I will message to you at your House tomorrow, before you depart."

You have had no time to be coopted, Arrhae thought

with some irony. *Well, now you have . . . no matter that it is happening at so high a level.* She wondered what she would be called upon to do with the data she would be acquiring . . . and how she was going to get out of this one, after they were finished with her. It was occurring to Arrhae at the moment that, as the most junior possible member of the Senate, she was probably also the most expendable member possible—no matter who she had been talking to, in what storeroom.

Nevertheless, she finished her cup of draft like a good guest, and stood, knowing a dismissal even if it was being much more politely handled than it would have been for a *hru'hfe.* "*Fvillha,*" she said, and bowed to him, "I am at your disposal in all ways."

"Until tomorrow then, *Deihu.*"

"Until tomorrow," Arrhae said. The door opened; a servant was standing there to see her out. On the steps under the portico, once more the honor guard was awaiting her, and its officer handed her into the waiting flitter and closed the door. A few moments later the flitter lifted itself up into the darkness, and the night took it.

So it was that *Deihu* Arrhae i-Khellian was sent off to spy on the Federation; and at the back of her mind, Terise Haleakala-LoBrutto, sent off years ago by the Federation to spy on the Romulans, found the jest very choice.

She could only hope, now, that it would not be the death of her.

* * *

15 Trianguli was one of those stars which had no particular interest for anyone except because of its position. It was a little type-K8 star, not quite small enough to qualify as a dwarf, orange-red, and planetless. There might have been an asteroid belt around it once, but if there had, long attrition had almost completely destroyed it. All this part of the Empire, on the far side of the Zone, shared the same dearth of resources; an unlucky chance for Ael's people, but one which circumstance and lack of resources elsewhere had forced them to ignore.

They had once come a long way out through this region, looking toward space which they could see had more stars, younger ones, stars big enough to have planets that could support hominid life. Unfortunately, it was Federation space they were looking at, those Rihannsu of nearly a century ago. Now this part of space was generally unintruded upon by either side, with the Zone not so far away . . . a desert again, untroubled, with nothing to attract anyone.

Except for now, as *Enterprise* and *Bloodwing* approached 15 Trianguli at warp five, preparing to drop out of warp well away from the star itself.

"T'Hrienteh?" Ael said, standing behind her center seat and studying the viewscreen, which showed stars and nothing else.

"Scan is flat," t'Hrienteh said, and t'Lamieh, her trainee, nodded agreement over her shoulder.

"But it would be," Ael said softly. She felt naked,

for *Bloodwing* was not cloaked; in *Enterprise's* company, it was for the moment unnecessary.

"Commander?" Jim's voice said.

"All seems clear, Captain," Ael said. "No sign of the Federation vessels as yet."

"They may be running a little behind," Jim said.

"It wouldn't be unusual, especially if our clocks really *are* out of synch. I've got to mention that to Starfleet. —Mr. Sulu, drop us out of warp. Decelerate to half impulse."

"The same," Ael said to Khiy, gripping the back of her chair.

The two ships dropped out of warp together, braking to dump down quickly out of the relativistic speeds. Ael swallowed . . .

. . . and saw, on the screen, at least one great twin-nacelled form shimmering out of cloak practically in front of them.

"*Evasive!*" Ael said to Khiy: but he had seen it before she did, and was already doing it. "Captain, ships decloaking——!"

"I see them," Jim said. "Company. *Lots* of company——"

The sweat broke out all over Ael to match what was already dampening her hands. Two or three ships, four or five, that she could have understood. But this flock of them, suddenly surrounding her, an open globe, tightening—it put her quite out of countenance.

Nevertheless she stood taller, put her shoulders

105

back, gripped the back of the chair, and grinned. There were still options. She thought gratefully now of how Khiy and Mr. Sulu had spent all that first night of meeting, before *Bloodwing* and *Enterprise* departed for these spaces, standing in one corner and making strange motions at one another in the air with their hands, so that they had to repeatedly put down their drinks to continue the conversation. Their crewmates from both sides had teased them about this at the time—all but Aidoann, who had been nearby, listening and watching them closely, and sent her a report on the exchange. It had all seemed quite farfetched at the time, and she had hoped it would not be necessary. Now, though, she would find out how farfetched it was. And as for the rest—

"Ds, *khre'Riov*," Aidoann said. "ChR 18, ChR 330, ChR 49, ChR 98, ChR 66, ChR 24, ChR 103—"

Arnie: Neirrh: Hmenna: Llemni: Orudain: all cruisers of *Bloodwing's* own class. And the big ones, the old supercruisers, *Ulitta* and *Madail.* None of them commanded by friends of hers, only the supercruisers better armed than *Bloodwing,* and the difference not so great considering the Klingon-sourced phaser conduits that had been clandestinely installed in her. But there were seven of them. "Not taking any chances, are they," said Jim's voice, remarkably calmly, from *Enterprise,* still outside the globe. "One of them leaving globe now, coming for us. Are any of these ships anybody you know, Commander?"

"Not personally," Ael said. "And at the moment, I fear we shall only meet in some other life."

"Still feeling insulted?"

"I will consult with you afterward as to that."

Jim laughed. "Understood. Implementing."

She swallowed. "Khiy," Ael said, "show us your mettle now——"

"Ie, khre'Riov," Khiy said.

The whole ship lurched sideways as he pulled *Bloodwing* around in a turn that made her structural field groan, and flung her straight at *Hmenna*, accelerating again toward warp, and firing like a mad thing, as if none of the rest of those ships closing in around them existed. They were basic enough tactics: to prevent englobement, pick a hole in the globe and escape. Sometimes it worked with one ship, sometimes it did not. *Hmenna* fired back, swelling in the screens——

——and then suddenly let loose a couple of hurried photon torpedoes and swung hastily away to port and "downward," as *Enterprise* came hurtling straight in at *Hmenna* from behind, as if planning to engage in a game of stones-crack-egg with *Bloodwing*, using *Hmenna* as the egg. The two of them passed at nearly the same moment through the gap left by *Hmenna*'s frantic movement with barely a third of a kilometer between them. *Bloodwing* went out of the globe through the gap: *Enterprise* went in and plunged straight across the inside of it, straight for *Madail*, pushing up through .9c and making for warp, though not firing, since using phasers at such transitional speeds can have unfortunate results.

Mad, he is mad! Ael thought. Maybe *Madaii* thought so too, for after a couple of ineffective phaser blasts at her shields she quickly moved sideways to let *Enterprise* out, rather than be rammed. Out *Enterprise* went, curving up high "over" the globe and down again, righting herself, making for the star.

Hmenna was after them now, and the globe was breaking up to follow. "Pay them no mind, Khiy," Ael said. "Do your business as it was agreed. Tr'Keirianh! Shields?"

"Holding, *khre'Riov,* but—"

"No buts," Ael said softly. "Do what you must, but hold them for your life, or that will prove short."

They headed straight for 15 Trianguli.

Jim sat watching *Bloodwing* as both ships broke into warp, and swallowed hard. "Mr. Sulu—"

"Well outside the critical warp radius, Captain," Sulu said. "Warp ingress went safely. No complications."

"Yet."

"I'm on it, Captain," Sulu said. "Warp two now. Khiy, you know the drill—"

"Will this work, Hikaru?" said Khiy's voice from *Bloodwing.*

"K8," Chekov said under his breath. "The star is marginal for the routine. Checking the spectroscopy—"

"No time for that now," Sulu said, and dove for it.

"There may not be enough mass," Chekov said. "It's borderline dwarf—"

"Captain?" Sulu said.

Jim breathed in, breathed out, clenched his hands on the arms of the center seat. "Seven of them. Two of us. Better find out," he said.

Enterprise and *Bloodwing* dove together for the star. Chekov was backing the bridge viewscreen's image intensity down as they went, but the glare was filling the bridge more unbearably every moment. Dwarf the star might be, "just a little K8," but this close to it, it started to look like Hell itself, and Jim found himself sweating and hoping he was not about to be in a position to make a much more detailed comparison. "Spock, what about the shields?"

"Holding," Spock said, peering down his viewer.

"No degradation. Tuning—" There was a pause, and then Spock said, "Shield tuning is showing some slide—"

Jim hit his comm switch. "Scotty," Jim said, "the shields are losing their tuning—"

There was a jangling from somewhere else in Engineering that began to shake, a bone-rattling vibration that combined very uncomfortably with the howl of the warp engines through *Enterprise*'s frame as she accelerated into the higher levels of warp. "Compensating," Scotty said, sounding tense. "The star's marginal, Captain! The corona's not as hot as

109

it ought to be, it's changing the way the field-tuning equations affect the shields——!"

"The paired iron lines are there," Chekov said suddenly. "Fe IX imaging is good. Working out the torpedo drop pattern now, *Bloodwing*——"

"Mr. Chekov, kindly hurry," Ael's voice said. "We seem to be having some difficulty with the tuning of our shields. If the ion wavefront hits us and we are not adequately protected——"

"Recompensating," Spock said. "Commander, here are better frequency-prediction algorithms for you. Transmitting. Use them to retune——"

"Got it," Chekov said softly. "Aidoann, here they come——"

A pause. "Evaluating," Aidoann's voice said, over an increasing engine roar from the other side. "Retuning shields now. Mr. Chekov, this means eight photon torpedoes for us at one per one-point-four Federation seconds. Coordinates plotting now——"

"Sounds right," Chekov said, eyeing the targeting viewer as it came up on his side of the helm. "Here comes the reception committee——"

"Fire aft, Mr. Chekov," Jim said. "Don't let them singe our tails!"

The pursuing ships were firing already, but with less and less effect as *Enterprise* and *Bloodwing* both dived closer to the sun; light-based weapons, even pumped to compensate for use in warp, are just as subject as any other kind of light to being bent out of true by the gravity well of a star. "Clean misses,"

Sulu said, sparing a moment from his piloting. "Ours too. Dropping out of warp to sublight. Coming down to ten thousand kilometers for the firing run—"

The ships chasing them were dropping out of warp and dropping back too, both unwilling to overshoot their prey and also unwilling to singe their own tails— possibly reasoning that *Bloodwing* and *Enterprise* could not keep this madness up forever. *And they're right,* Jim thought; for though the ships' shields were being tailored to cope with high-speed ionic discharge, there was little they could do about simple radiant heat . . . and it was getting hot already. "Scotty, how much time can we spend here?" Jim said.

"Twenty-four seconds total," Scotty said. "Plus or minus two. After that the hull will start to buckle—"

Jim held on to the arms of his seat, while the front viewscreen, turned down as low as it could go without actually being turned off, was still blazing with the furious dark orange fire of 15 Tri. Ahead of them, a scarcely seen black blot against the rolling "rice-grain" plasma structure of the star's low atmosphere, *Bloodwing* was skimming even lower than they were over the photosphere, firing photon torpedoes off to both sides, into the "base" of the star's corona. "Phaser program starts now," Chekov said, and hit his controls.

The *Enterprise's* phasers stitched through the star's corona, flickering, the fire looking almost continuous, but not quite, like the flicker in old-fashioned neon tubes that Jim had seen. Chains of sunspots abruptly began to bubble blackly up all over the star's surface, responding to the changes being induced in the uppermost part of the star's magnetic field. "Dark sprite effect," Chekov said. "Base percentage reached—"

"Uhura," Jim said, hanging on as the ship began to shudder more violently, and sparing a hand from holding on to wipe the sweat off his forehead, "elapsed time?"

"Eighteen seconds, Captain."

It felt like eighteen years. "Preparing for warp eleven," Sulu said. "Accelerating out of the gravity well now."

"Back in a moment, *Bloodwing*," Jim said. The ship was cooling again, but that would not last. Out they went into the dark, and three of the seven ships came after them.

"Warp two. Warp three. Pursuit is in warp and accelerating."

"Ready on the aft phaser banks, Mr. Chekov. Prepare a spread of torpedoes."

"Ready, Captain."

"Warp five," Sulu said. "Warp six. Turning." Everything slewed sideways: the ship was groaning softly now, the skinfield complaining about the stresses being applied to it . . . and worse was to come.

"Aft view," Jim said. The screen flickered. Jim saw two of the pursuing Romulan vessels trying to turn to match, but not doing as well: turning wide, losing ground. The third one, the biggest of them, was turning and gaining on them, and firing.

"Clean misses. Warp eight," Sulu said. Suddenly 15 Trianguli was swelling to fill the screen, flashing toward them. "Warp nine——"

"Mind that helm, mister," Jim said softly.

"Warp ten. She's steady, Captain," Sulu said, while the ship began to shake and her structural members to howl in a way that suggested Sulu's definition of *steady* was a novel one.

"Captain—" Scotty's voice called out from the comm.

"Duly noted, Mr. Scott," Jim answered calmly, never taking his eyes off Sulu at the helm.

"High photosphere. Warp eleven—!"

Enterprise's engines roared; the ship lurched as it hit the star's "near" bowshock, lurched again, and then began to accelerate powerfully around the tight end of a "cometary" hyperbolic curve with the star at its focus. The sun's corona, already irritated by the photon torpedoes and tuned phaser fire, was now pierced straight through by the carefully deformed warp field of a starship doing warp eleven . . . .

. . . and nothing happened. 15 Trianguli's cor-ona lashed furiously at them as they whipped around and flashed away, but there was no burst of sudden ion-ization. The ship following them most closely, *Madain*, began to fire again. *Enterprise* shuddered.

"A hit on the port nacelle," Spock said. "Shields down fifteen percent."

113

"They won't take that kind of thing for long!" Scotty's voice came from the engine room. "All those laddies have to do is keep firing at us, eventually they'll get lucky—"

"The stellar atmosphere is insufficiently stimulated," Spock said. "Another pass—"

"Mr. Spock, we *can't*—"

"The warp-field incursion effect has not yet attenuated," Spock said. "It will last another eight point six seconds. *Bloodwing*—"

"Mr. Spock!" Ael said. "We seem somewhat short of results here!"

"If you will make one more sweep at ten thousand kilometers, with phasers tuned a third higher than ours—"

"Do it, Khiy!" Jim heard Ael say.

"Implementing—"

They plunged outward and away from the star. "View aft!" Jim said. The Romulan ship that had been chasing them was still doing so, firing still. They were keeping ahead of it, but it was starting to catch up as they watched *Bloodwing* dive low toward the chromosphere one more time. Overstimulated ions trailed behind her in a million-degree contrail from which *Bloodwing* was preserved only by its tenuousness. "For God's sake be careful," Jim said softly. The last thing any of them needed right this moment was for *Bloodwing* to be thrown back in time. Her phasers lanced out into the corona, flickering nearly as steadily as *Enterprise*'s had—

The star's corona wavered around her, went sickly and pallid, and collapsed.

Jim swallowed. *"Bloodwing, get out of there!"*

She angled around and upward, arrowed away from the star. They all saw it start to come, then: a secondary curve of faint light over the surface of 15 Trianguli, not orange but bizarrely blue, rearing up right across the body of the star, like a bubble blowing—but a bubble nearly as big as the star was, easily two-thirds of its diameter. "Here it comes!," Sulu cried, and hit the ship's impact alarms.

The screech of them went through everything. "All hands, brace for impact!!" Jim shouted, and braced himself as best he could, knowing that his odds of staying where he was were no better than fifty-fifty. "Maximum warp, Mr. Sulu, now or never!!"

The bubble continued to bend itself up and up from the star's chromosphere, arching, inflating, its "surface" swirling like that of a soap bubble with that virulent blue glow—getting taller all the time, impossibly tall, compared to the star. Any spicule, any prominence, would long since have either fallen back into the chromosphere, or blown away entirely . . . but not this thing. It *grew*. From Engineering, over the roar of the engines, he heard a voice like a very nervous xylophone saying, "Dear Archictetrix, Sc'tty, look at it, it's not supposed to do *that—!"*

Oh, wonderful, Jim thought. *"Bloodwing—!"*

"Right behind you, Captain," Ael's voice said. But

they were *not* right behind *Enterprise*: they were well behind. *If their shields aren't tuned properly*—

The other Rihannsu ships had seen that upward-straining shape and in seven different directions, and fled.

Blue, bulging, awful, the bubble strained outward . . . and then the bubble burst.

The Sunseed effect, as K's't'lk had said, released so much energy into such a small volume of space at such a speed and intensity that much of it had no choice but to propagate into subspace as a sleet of stripped ions, cyclotron radiation, and other subatomic particles. Once there, the newly created ion storm did not go faster than light itself, but it affected anything in subspace that did, such as ships with warp fields. The effect, so close to its source, was as if a great hand had grabbed *Enterprise* and was trying to use it for a saltshaker. Jim hung on tight, grimly determined that even if he died right now, he was going to do it in his command chair and not rolling around on the floor.

But dying was apparently not in the cards. The shaking began to ease off. Jim stared into the screen and saw eight sparks of light scattered over a great area of space behind him, all of them brilliantly backlit by an orange star, suddenly abnormally bright, with an equally sudden, swiftly expanding spherical halo of dimming but deadly blue-white fire. That halo expanded to meet them, surrounded them, rushed past them—

Seven of them flowered into fire themselves, one

after another, as their shields failed, and in both realspace and subspace a billion tons of plasma struck them at a temperature of nearly two million degrees. The little spheres of pure white fire produced by the instantaneous annihilation of all the matter and antimatter in what remained of their warp engines was briefly hotter; but not by much, and not for long.

And one spark burned bright for a moment, its tuned shields shrieking light . . . then dull again, and duller still as the star behind it began to recover from its very brief solar flare.

"*Bloodwing,*" Jim said.

Silence.

"*Enterprise,*" Ael said, after a moment.

Jim breathed out. "Is everyone all right over there?"

"My nerves are a casualty, I would say," Ael said. "But the shields held, for which I praise Fire's name . . . having seen It so close to hand, and lived. We have some minor structural problems, I believe."

"We too will need to examine the hull, Captain," Spock said. "But initial indicators seem to suggest only minor damage."

"Good. Let's get it taken care of," Jim said, and stood up, now that it was safe to do so. "Scotty, K's't'lk, nice work."

"Thank you, Captain," Scotty said.

"I must apologize, Captain," K's't'lk said. "I had hoped for better."

Jim paused. "Sorry?"

"There was supposed to be a lovely evenly generated ionization effect that propagated right around the corona," K's't'lk said, sounding mournful. "Not just a coronal mass ejection like that, all lumpy and asymmetrical."

"I thought it worked rather well," Ael said, sounding dubious.

"But not the way it was supposed to," K's't'lk said. "Captain, Commander, I am mortified. We were very nearly all roast."

"You mean toast," Sulu said.

"Toast, thank you."

"Nonetheless," Ael said, "we are all alive . . . a situation on which I would have been unwilling to suggest odds when I first saw what was waiting for us. If a few adjustments in your version of the process need to be made, well, that is the history of science. But meantime, the effectiveness of the tuned-shield approach against the Sunseed routines is very neatly proven."

"Assuming one knows the frequencies to which the shields must be tuned ahead of time," Spock said. "Assessing and tuning them when the star cannot be analyzed ahead of time, but must be assessed at the *same* time, will be a considerable challenge."

"I leave that to the three of you," Jim said. "Meanwhile, we have another problem. There were seven Romulan ships in Federation space when they had no business to be there. I don't suppose that was the diplomatic mission. . . ."

"If it was, we have committed nearly as serious a breach of protocol as they did," Ael said dryly. "But

I very much doubt they had anything to do with the ships we are still expecting."

"So do I," Jim sighed and rubbed his face. "Lieutenant Uhura, prepare a message with a record of what just happened here and prepare to send it off to Starfleet, suitably encrypted." For the moment he was willing to put his concerns about possibly broken encryption aside: if the Romulans could decode this message, let them. It would give them something to think about. "No technical details for the moment, though: keep it dry. Let me see it when it's done: I'll be in my quarters for a little while."

"Bridge?"

Jim punched the comm button again. "Problems, Bones?"

"Nothing serious, but I'm glad you told me to fasten things down, down here. What the devil was *that?*"

"I'll have Uhura send you down a recording to view at your leisure," Jim said, and grinned. Now that it was over, grinning was possible again.

"Thanks loads. Out."

Jim turned to Spock. "Mr. Spock, when is the task force due?"

"Twenty-eight hours and eighteen minutes from now, Captain."

"Very well. Let's get whatever repairs need to be done out of the way, and take the evening off. Keep the shields up, though, except as necessary. Commander, perhaps some of your crew would join us for dinner, and afterward."

119

"Our pleasure, Captain."

"Excellent. Maybe you would call me in my quarters in a few minutes? There are some things we should discuss."

"Certainly, Captain. Out."

Jim got up, went into the lift, and tried to order his thoughts. After a pell-mell encounter like the one of the last few minutes, sometimes this took a while. But he busied himself with one of the breathing exercises Bones had taught him, and shut his eyes while the lift hummed along, concentrating on seeing space as a calm place again, full of cold and silence and the fierce pale light of the stars. By the time the lift doors slid open again, things were better . . . except in one regard.

The call was waiting on his viewer when he came in and sat down in front of it. At the sound of his movement, Ael looked up. She had moved down to her own cabin from *Bloodwing's* bridge.

"So you were right," she said, "about the ambush."

"And so were you."

"I? I did nothing but agree with you."

"True." Jim leaned his elbows on the desk, laced his fingers together, and put his chin on them. "And without discussion. Which suggests to me that you had previously had your suspicions as well . . . which you did not exactly spell out to me."

She went quiet at that. "I dislike being thought merely paranoid," Ael said.

"You also dislike being wrong," said Jim.

"Yes," Ael said, "but more lives than mine, or mine and *Bloodwing*'s, are on the line here. Various people's actions in the Empire will be powerfully influenced by ours . . . and many innocents may live or die according to what those people do, when news of what has happened to us will make it back to the Two Worlds."

"It won't be brought back by *those* ships."

"No." There was a brief pause. "Even now, Jim, even after what we went through at Levaeri, when my son, my own son, turned traitor and tried to take your ship, and he and all the people who turned with him suffered the penalty for such betrayal——even after that, I still believe there are still most likely agents of the Empire aboard my ship; crew who did not reveal their affinities then, but conceal them still, passing messages back to ch'Rihan when they can. I did not dare generally reveal my thoughts about what might be waiting for *Bloodwing* at 15 Trianguli if we had kept to the original schedule; and I did not tell my crew at large that we were going to divert to Hamal first, or that we would leave it accompanied, instead of going alone to 15 Tri. Now behold what has happened . . . for *Bloodwing* comes to the spot where it was intended to wait alone, and finds seven Rihannsu ships waiting. And now no ship will go home to ch'Rihan to tell what happened; which is a good thing."

"Commander," Jim said.

Her eyes widened a little at his tone.

"How the *hell* am I supposed to trust you," Jim said, "if you won't trust *me?*"

She made no answer to that right away. After a moment, Ael glanced down at her desk. "I see that I have done you an injustice," she said. "Habit . . . can be very difficult to break."

"Something for you to talk to your chief surgeon about, maybe," Jim said. He was angry, but he wasn't going to let that affect him any more than necessary. "God forbid I should criticize you for calculating . . . your calculation has saved both our lives, once or twice. But there's no reason for you to do it *alone*. Especially when it's my crew's lives on the line, as well."

She was silent.

"In the meantime, I was right, and you were right, to take the course of action we did. And you're right about this too: regardless of how many spies may still be aboard *Bloodwing*, we now have enough evidence for my own purposes that there are intelligence leaks fairly high up in Starfleet, and those leaks are reaching straight back to ch'Rihan. Very few people at our end of things knew when you were supposed to be at 15 Tri, alone, to meet the task force that will shortly be arriving. My problem is that, after what's happened, they'll know that *I* have reason to suspect those leaks. This may translate into a loss of advantage for me, depending on how high up the leaks go . . . and I'm damned if I know what to do about it."

"They will not know that," Ael said, "if I tell them that *I* convinced you to accompany *Bloodwing* there." Jim opened his mouth. "They will half believe that anyway, Jim; for Starfleet cannot at the best of times be very sanguine about our association. Certainly they must look at it and see all manner of things that are not there."

Jim closed his mouth again. After a moment he said, "Interesting idea."

"And this I will be glad to do when the task force arrives," Ael said. "It seems like the least I can do . . . by way of apology."

Their eyes met. After a second, Jim let out a breath. "Let's see if it's genuinely necessary," he said. "Very well."

"Meanwhile," Jim said, "the presence of those ships themselves are evidence that you were right in more than one way. There *will* be a war, now. Their presence in Federation space, without permission given beforehand for the transit, was itself an act of war according to the terms of the treaty which established the Zone . . . which tells me that someone in your government is getting ready to throw that treaty right out the window, no matter *what* Starfleet decides to do about you and *Bloodwing* and the Sword. From our two points of view, that certainly is going to change things."

"Yes," Ael said softly. "It will."

"I want to discuss this with you further," Jim said. "But let's leave that for this evening, when your crew are here as well. That way there'll be a little less notice taken when you spend a good while talking to me . . . in places where we can't be overheard, by your crew *or* mine."

Jim raised his eyebrows. "Why, thank you, I think." he flushed. "Not like *that*," he said crossly.

"Indeed not," Ael said. "The thought was furthest from my mind."

She briefly gave him a rather wicked look. Jim raised his eyebrows. "Why, thank you, I think."

"You are very welcome. What time shall I begin the leaves, Jim?"

"A couple of hours." She reached out for the control for her viewer.

"Ael," he said.

She paused, looking at him thoughtfully.

" . . . It's all right."

Ael's eyes dwelt on him for a moment more. "That must yet be seen," she said, and she bowed her head, and cut the connection.

Jim sat there for a while, frowning, thinking. *She may not be alone in the doing-an-injustice department*, he thought. *Think of the shock of being betrayed, not just by a co-officer, but by your own son.* The thought was profoundly uncomfortable; he wanted to turn away from it, but forced himself to face it regardless. The loyalty of his officers and crew, not unquestioning but utterly reliable, was something Jim had come to take for granted, like air to breathe. He could not conceive of life on *Enterprise* without it. Ael, though, having had something very like that with her own crew, had now seen that seemingly solid ground fall away from under her feet. And across that suddenly shifting, crumbling landscape, she was now walking into what would be, if Jim was right in his guesses, the greatest challenge of her career: if indeed she considered that she had a "career" left as such. At any rate, it was a situation from which she would emerge alive and triumphant—or dead. He could still hear that proud, cool voice saying, "Flight would not be my choice . . . it will solve nothing." One way or another, unresolved details aside . . . she was still resolved to fight. And all this without knowing, any longer, if she could completely trust her own crew.

Once burned . . . Jim thought. But it all still comes down to trust. If this situation is to be survivable— she's got to learn to trust me.

And can she ever?

He sighed, then got up and went off to have a shower, and see about a meal.

Chapter Four

MANY LIGHT-YEARS away from 15 Trianguli, two men sat in a dim-lit room, awaiting the arrival of a third. The two scowling around them at the high-ceilinged, tapestried, weapon-hung surroundings, which were unusally rich and splendid even as high-caste Klingons reckoned such things, a twilight of crimson and dully gleaming gold. The two Klingons were also scowling at one another, for normally, had they met in the street, they would have attacked one another.

There was blood feud between Kelg's house and Kurvad's, a feud that both houses had cultivated with pleasure for a decade. Unfortunately, the house in which the two enemies now sat was senior to both of theirs by centuries, and the man whom they awaited was so high-caste that any feud must needs be set aside until they had discharged whatever errand he might set the two of them. The necessity did not make the waiting any easier, though, and the silence between them was broken by the occasional snarl. That, at least, propriety permitted. Kelg entertained himself with thoughts of what else he would do, some time soon, when circumstances brought him and Kurvad together in some less ritually restrictive environment.

For nearly half an hour they had to sit in the dimness, waiting. Somewhere nearby the noon meal had been served, and Kelg's gut growled at the smell of choice viands, the smoky hint of *saltha* on the air, the scent of bloodwine. But nothing was offered them. Kelg sat there fuming at the insult until the great black carved doors swung open, and K'hemren walked in. Kelg and Kurvad stood to greet him, then sat down again.

"I will hear your report," said K'hemren, reaching behind his tall chair. The scent of the feast to which they had not been invited swirled in the air around them as the doors to K'hemren's counseling chamber closed.

"They are finally moving," said Kelg, determined to speak the first word at this meeting in Kurvad's despite, and as much intent on drowning any sound his gut might make. "And doing it with surprising openness. No hiding it . . . no cover stories."

"Beware the *targ* without a bone in his mouth,"

said Kurvad, sneering, "and the Romulan without a lie in his."

"The cliché is true enough," said Kelg. "And what are we to make of what they are doing? Not what they *want* us to, surely?"

K'hemren had brought out from behind the tall chair a long, curved, extremely handsome *bat'leth*. This he now laid in his lap. "It is toward the Federation that they move," he said, glancing up. "And some interesting pieces of news have come to us, through their own news services, and even via messages routed through our own message networks."

Kelg and Kurvad looked at him curiously, but he did not elaborate. Finally Kurvad said, "The archtraitress whom they've all been yelping about the last couple of months apparently has gone to ground in Federation space. Seems that she may either be about to ask them for asylum, or else she has done so already . . . I am none too clear on the details."

Kelg, laughing at him, got up and began to pace. "They will never give it to her! She would become an occasion of war, and if there is one thing they never want, it is a war!"

"She has already become such an occasion," said K'hemren, thoughtfully stroking the *bat'leth*, "and she is indeed now in their hands. Yet they have not sent her back across the Zone, which would have been the most straightforward response." He smiled slightly. "But there is a reason for that, it seems."

Kelg paused. He and Kurvad looked at K'hemren curiously.

"She has been with Kirk," K'hemren said, "in *Enterprise.*"

Kurvad spat on the floor and leaped to his feet, beginning to pace as well, though at the mandated safe distance from Kelg. "I thought ill enough of human manners," he growled, "but the man mates with aliens, with animals, as well? It is intolerable——"

"...that one who behaves so, nonetheless also beats every ship of ours he meets?" K'hemren looked down at the *bat'leth* in amusement. "Maybe so. But his victories cannot be denied him—may the last Dark only devour him soon."

"That the two of them should be conniving together—" said Kelg. "It bodes ill for someone."

"The Romulans, I think," said K'hemren. "That one does not love her people: she has betrayed them before. So she meets with Kirk, as before, to hatch out some new betrayal." He smiled slightly. "But then she is a madwoman. Her niece was betrayed by Kirk and his half-breed first officer, and yet the woman blames her own people for what happened to the niece. Irrational."

Kelg stood still for a moment, thinking about that irrationality and what might be made of it, if the circumstances were right. The woman had been deadly enough in her way: the thought of somehow pushing Kurvad into her path was amusing. "One could wish she would only turn on Kirk some fine morning and tear his throat out," said Kurvad.

"It would be too much to ask of the Universe," said K'hemren. "Meanwhile, these ship movements . . ."

"They concern me," said Kelg, beginning to pace again, though more slowly now. "The Romulans would not dare move toward battle unless they had acquired something which made them completely fearless."

"You underestimate them," said Kurvad. "They have the strength to conduct a little border war, surely. . . ."

Kelg sneered at the idea, typical of Kurvad's witlessness and cowardice, and was amused by Kurvad's outraged look. "Have they indeed! They didn't react to our attack on Khashah IV—what is it they call it? Eilhaunn? They withdrew their forces, they *let* us take it!"

"A trick. While they do that on the one hand, on the other they move directly into Federation space—"

"With all of seven ships!"

"Do you think me a complete fool!? There have been many more ship movements than that in Romulan space near where the Zone meets Federation space, over the past tenday and a half. And similar movements where the Zone comes close to our own space! Once again they use the Zone to cloak their own movements. And their new cloaking device is in use as well; who knows what they are letting us see just to distract us from what we can't see elsewhere?"

Kelg laughed again. "There are no great strategists among them . . ."

"There do not have to be!" K'hemren roared. Kelg stopped, shocked still for the moment. "They are afraid!—which makes them dangerous. And more, they have no hope!"

K'hemren's vehemence silenced both Kelg and Kurvad for a moment. "We have closed down our relations with them much too tightly in recent months," he said. "Now they have no hope in dealing with us . . . and one should never leave one's enemy without hope. First of all because it is a weapon in one's own hand, sunk in their guts, which one can twist when one needs to. But secondly because an enemy without hope swiftly becomes an enemy with nothing to lose!"

It was good sense in its way, but Kelg was reluctant to admit this. "The Emperor," he muttered, "is not going to have much patience for these philosophical discussions. He is going to want to know how many more planets we have taken since we spoke to him last. It does not take a Thought Admiral to see that the present answer will not please him."

K'hemren shrugged, studying the *bat'leth*'s steel, and turned it over in his lap. "Even the Emperor cannot have everything his own way," he said. "It would be a fool's act to attack any more worlds before hostilities break out. Let the fog of war descend first. Under its cover, many attacks can take place, and no one will know whose responsibility they are."

"No one who does not bother analyzing the ion trails and residues," said Kurvad.

"Kurvad, are you *entirely* without a spleen?" Kelg cried, taking a few steps toward the other, but not so many as to come close enough to him to entitle him to retaliate physically. "There will be no time for forensics when this war breaks out in earnest! Our business now is to designate targets for when it *does* break. We need metals, heavy and light; and we need slave labor. Those we will be able to get in plenty from the worlds around our bridgehead at Eilhaunn."

He did not add what use his house, involved in the attack on that planet, would be able to make of those resources; they would shortly be rich, and the riches would buy them the influence with the Emperor's advisers that they had never been able to afford before. After that, the Romulans could go to whatever hell they preferred: Kelg's house would have more important things to think about. *Maybe even, some-day, the seat of Empire itself—* "The damned Romu-lans will have their hands full with the Federation, anyway. They are concentrating most of their forces on that side of the Zone."

"Not all of them—"

"All the ones that would cause us trouble! And the Federation is taking the bait, moving their own ships into that quadrant as well. Now at last comes our chance to take back much of what was left in the Federation's hands when the curst Organians interfered. The Federation has left their flank too un-guarded. Only a little while more of ship movements like this, in which they seek to overawe their enemy and keep him from fighting, and they will have un-balanced themselves enough so that the enemy which *does* want to fight will be able to move in and start a real war, not this pitiful little border skirmish!" He spat on the floor again and turned away; seen only as a shadow, a slave crept in to mop up the spittle.

Somewhere distant in the great house, voices were lifted in song: cups could be heard clanking, at that feast to which Kelg had not been invited. *But that will change. Soon the feasts of triumph will begin, and I shall be foremost at them all—and Kur-vad's skull will be bound in steel and used as a spit-toon.* "What else have you to report, then?" said K'hemren.

"Nothing else," said Kelg. "When must we re-turn?"

"I don't know," said K'hemren. "I must first speak with the Emperor. Go back to your fleets and get them ready for battle. I will contact you when he has orders for you."

"Will it be war?"

"I think that will probably be unavoidable," said Khemren, with a smile.

Kelg and Kurvad did the only thing they could conceivably have done together: they leapt up from their chairs and shouted for victory. K'hemren stayed seated, stroking the *bat'leth*'s pattern-welded steel.

133

"Yes," he said, "you will have your chance at both the Romulans and the Federation, I make no doubt. But beware lest some unhappy fate throws you in the path of Kirk and that bitch-traitress of his."

"It would be no unhappy fate for me," said Kelg. "My brother served with Kang, and came to grief at Kirk's hands." The images of what revenge he might take if the man ever crossed his path had long been the delight of his idle moments. Now, there was at least a chance that they might come true.

"And my cousin," said Kurvad, "when he served with Koloth: the same."

K'hemren said nothing. "Go back to your ships," he said, "and wait."

Kelg glared at K'hemren for just a second or so, for he had not declared their errand complete: they could not try to kill each other, as they had been longing to do. *But there'll be another day,* Kelg thought. *Is not war full of unfortunate accidents?* He headed out of the room with only a single angry glance at Kurvad.

Behind him, as the door shut, he caught a last glimpse of K'hemren: not hurrying out to his interrupted feast, but sitting quietly in the chair, in the dimness, stroking the *bat'leth,* thinking.

That evening there were a lot of people in the rec deck. There was no special event arranged—nothing but the usual scatter of games, conversation, occasional music or song, and people moving around and eating and drinking casually. Still, Jim could, after long experience, feel the tension in the air—the sense of there having been a very close call—and could also feel it discharging itself. But this was what Rec was for, at its best: this was one of the reasons why the Recreation Department was classified as part of Medicine, and reported directly to McCoy. McCoy was in fact here as well, as much for his own discharge of tension as to keep an eye on everyone else—though which reason was more important to him, Jim thought he knew.

There were, as Jim had intended, a fair number of Rihannsu in attendance—though for Starfleet's peace of mind, and indeed Jim's, they were all in here, and not wandering around his ship without supervision. The food processors were proving extremely popular, and when Jim came down from the balcony where he had been keeping an eye on things to greet Ael shortly after she entered, he found her standing with a disappointed look next to one of them. To K's't'lk, beside her, Ael was saying, "It is rather unfortunate. I have something of a savory tooth, and *kheia* is very choice . . . and something we could not normally afford to have on *Bloodwing*, I can tell you that."

"Problems?" Jim said.

"My crew, the greedy *hlai*, have eaten all the *kheia*," Ael said. She glanced over at Aidoann, who was standing nearby with a pair of tongs and a plate that was very nearly empty. "Is this *mnhei'sahe*, then? To starve your commander?"

Aidoann shot Jim an amused look, and then held out her plate, and her tongs, handles first, to Ael. "We exist to serve," she said. Laughter came from the various other crew around her, Khiy and tr'Keirianh the master engineer, who were eating just as fast as they could and seemed in no rush to make gestures of self-sacrifice.

"Oh, away with you," Ael said, laughing. "There are more than enough other dainties. Just look here; see the size of this *llsathis!* Here, I will have a slice of that, and just a cup of ale, and leave the *kheia* to my poor starving children." Her people laughed at her lofty tone, apparently not at all fooled by it.

"Allow me," Jim said, and cut her a slice of what appeared to be a giant blue gelatin ring. "Ael, why is so much of your food blue?"

She blinked as she took the plate and a spoon. They strolled away from the table, K's't'lk coming with them with a plate held up on two of her back legs. "Why should it not be?"

"It's not a very usual color for us."

"Perhaps. But one person's usual is another man's odd, I should think. Surely it would not be usual for you to eat . . . Forgive me, madam, but what *is* that?"

"Graphite," K's't'lk said, picking up another chunk of it as they walked, and bringing it close to her body. Jim didn't see where it went—he never had, where solid foods were concerned—and he had given up staring to try to find out. "I am off duty now, and may permit myself to indulge a little."

"It is an intoxicant?"

"For us, yes." She gave Jim a look out of what was currently the frontmost cluster of eyes. "And all too often present company has encouraged me to indulge, when we were in private."

"You're interesting when you start getting atonal," Jim said, "that's all."

K's't'lk chimed at him in major ninths, a sarcastic but still good-natured sound. "You two are old intimates, then," Ael said, "and do not merely work together."

"Oh yes. Many a long quiet talk the captain and I have had in his quarters," K's't'lk said, "about life and the universe. But that cabin is famous across the quadrant, Commander. Beware how you go!"

"Why," Ael said calmly, "what should happen to me there?"

Jim looked at K's't'lk with mock outrage. "You're a fine one to talk," he said, "after what *you* did in my quarters!"

"What did she do?" Ael said.

Jim opened his mouth, shut it again, then laughed. "I'm not sure exactly how to describe it," he said.

"*H't'r'tk'tv'mtk*," K's't'lk said, or sang. "The term has no close equivalent among hominid species, Commander. I reproduced myself."

"What," Ael said, "right *there?*"

Those blue-burning eyes, full of their shifting fires, dwelt on Jim again with some amusement. "Certainly it's not something one would do just *any-*

137

place," K's't'lk said. "It needs a secure environment. A certain amount of intellectual and emotional engagement. . . . And shelves."

"Oh, well, thank you very much," Jim said, nonplussed. " 'Shelves.' " Then he laughed. "You two really should get together sometime and discuss it further. Meanwhile, T'l—what about 15 Trianguli?"

"I was hoping you wouldn't mention that."

"Somebody has to," Jim said. "That star didn't behave as advertised."

"In a manner of speaking it did," K's't'lk said, sounding even more embarrassed. "The only reason the technique didn't work correctly was that, as Mr. Chekov mentioned at the time, the star is only marginally a candidate for being seeded. If it had been just a very little more massive, or a touch hotter, say a K6, we would have gotten a smooth propagation of the ion-storm effect into subspace, instead of a coronal mass ejection, which was not what I had in mind. A thing like that could kill you."

Jim and Ael exchanged a look over her back. "But certainly," Ael said, "this experience will have provided you with valuable data for more accurately establishing your baselines in the future."

"Commander," K's't'lk said, "you are a gracious lady, and I thank you for trying to make me feel better. But, I'm, I apologize to you. Once more I have put your ship in danger by not adequately predicting all the variables in a situation."

"Oh, come on, T'l . . ." Jim said. "You did what you

could with what you had; it wasn't as if you could have sent that star back and got a better one. And we all came out of it well enough; consider this a minor setback. What *did* work brilliantly was the shields."

"Yes, they did function nicely, didn't they," K's't'lk said. She sounded slightly more cheerful. "The only problem was the way we had to keep retuning them separately on both ships."

Ael's expression became puzzled. "I am not sure how that could be avoided. The ships are after all discrete entities, each with its own warp signature and structure, requiring different tuning for each warp field's shape."

"Oh, of course," K's't'lk said, "but for joint operations like this it would be more elegant to have only one mechanism handling both sets of tuning." She chimed softly for a moment. "You know," she said then, "if you . . . No."

"No?" Ael said.

"No, it would just bring in the equivalence heresy," K's't'lk said, "and hard on the heels of *that* come all kinds of quantum uncertainties as well. Unresolved energy-state phyla, subspace phase-shift intransigences. There are enough of those already." She sighed, a sound like minor-chord windchimes.

"T'l," Jim said, "you were supposed to be enjoying yourself a little, here. And look, you've run out of graphite."

"Don't tempt me. Now, *intransigences* . . ." K's't'lk said, in a rather different tone of voice. "Now *there's* an interesting thought. I should go talk to Sc'ty. Captain, Commander, if you'd excuse me——"

K's't'lk went jangling off across the room at speed.

"Now you've done it," Jim said, watching her go.

"I have done it?"

Jim chuckled as they walked away. "I take it," Ael said, "you are well used to not being clear about what she is discussing."

"You have no idea. The things she's done to my ship——" He smiled. "Well, I'll forgive her a great deal; the results have sometimes been spectacular. Come on, Ael, let's sit down and relax."

He led her up to the balcony at the top of the recreation deck, nearest the great windows, where a few chairs and tables had been set out. *Bloodwing* had little in the way of ports, Jim knew; and he knew the impulse to bring her up here had been the correct one as she stood there and looked out the huge clearsteel windows, silently, her food momentarily forgotten.

"There's an observation deck above this one," Jim said. "Quieter, if you prefer it——"

"No," Ael said, "this suits me well enough. I have had enough quiet and solitude over the last couple of months; this makes a pleasant change . . . even if the voices breaking the silence, some of them, are strange."

They sat down and watched the mingling crews beneath them for a while, during which time Ael demolished the blue gelatin-stuff on her plate, and Jim sat cradling the old port which McCoy, now down there talking to tr'Hrienteh, had handed him on his way over to greet Ael. Finally the two of them were left sipping their respective drinks, while beneath them people chatted and sang and laughed and played quiet games, and the evening slipped by.

Jim wasn't sure how long they had been up there, discussing this and that, before Harb Tanzer was coming up the steps toward them. "Captain," he said, "Commander, can I get you anything?"

"Ael?" Jim said.

She shook her head. "I am in comfort," she said. "It has been a pleasure to be here, for a change, when hostilities were not in progress." Her voice was a touch sad: Jim could practically hear her thinking, *As they are about to be again.*

Harb only nodded. "Yes," he said. "The last time you were here, there wasn't much time for recreation as such. This place . . ." He looked around, plainly seeing it as it had been once when the corridors outside had been full of Romulans suddenly turned treacherous, and the inside was full of *Enterprise* crew and Romulans friendly to them, but unarmed. "This place," Harb said finally, "got to be a mess." He looked around it now, gazing at the crewpeople, human and Rihannsu and many others, who were milling around eating and drinking and talking. "It's much improved now."

There was a faint rumbling through the floor, and Harb looked up as Mr. Naraht came in. "Aha," Harb said. "Captain, Commander, would you excuse me? I want to go see what he thinks of the new batch of granite."

"Go on, Mr. Tanzer," Jim said. "I'll be pleased to hear."

He went on down into the crowd on the main floor, which was thinning somewhat now as the evening went on: the day had taken its toll on everyone. "Ael," Jim said after a few moments. "We can't leave it much longer. They're going to be here tomorrow."

"I know," she said softly.

"So tell me now. What are you going to do?"

Ael sighed, a heavy sound; and it came to Jim that he had never heard her sigh before, or at least couldn't remember it. "Only this," she said. "I think I must lead a force of ships and ground troops back to ch'Rihan and ch'Havran, and meet the forces of my homeworlds in battle . . . with an eye to unseating the government."

"Oh," Jim said.

She gave him a look. "Aye, I hear you thinking: 'Where is she keeping this force? I have not seen it.' Well, nor have I. But it is there, and growing . . . if my sources tell me true. And I believe they do."

"If they don't," Jim said, "you're going to be in for a very interesting time."

"I am in for that regardless," Ael said.

"Your government's been in place a long while," Jim said. "I doubt it's just going to let you walk in and topple it." *And what if she thinks it will? . . . We may be in big trouble. . . .*

She sat back and folded her arms. "In the older days," Ael said, "what you say would unquestionably have been true. Its strength was better distributed, then. But now it grows top-heavy, and therein lies both the source of some of our troubles as a people, and their solution."

She got a brooding look. "It is not so much the Senate with which I quarrel," Ael said. "It works well enough. But the Praetorate has acquired far more power than it used to have in the days when it was mostly our high judiciary, ruling on finer points of the law which the Senate had passed and the Expunging Body could not muster enough of a majority to remove. Now, for various reasons of expediency and habit, the Praetorate has begun to sway the Senate itself, pushing the power blocs which compose it into what directions they please. In some cases I suspect it—as do others—of encouraging the formation of those blocs itself, to make the Senate as a whole easier to manipulate. 'Independent' senators are few and far between, these days, and those who choose to remain so for long are either blind to the forces moving around them, or stubborn enough not to care. A senator unaligned with one of the major power blocs is all too likely to become suspect, attracting the attention of Intelligence or other unfriendly organizations subject to the Praetorate's dictates. All too soon senators who realize this tend to fall into line."

Jim turned that over in his mind. *What a mess. . . . But he had not missed her annoyed tone.* This was plainly something Ael would very much like to do something about. "I get the sense from what you're saying that the Praetorate itself has its own blocs."

Ael nodded. "And therein lies the problem. There are only twelve praetors, and when so much power is concentrated in so few hands, trouble inevitably starts. Once upon a time all praetors came of houses of great power and wealth, so much so—it was thought—that they would not need to strive one against another in the political realm. But too little of Rihannsu nature the lawmakers knew who believed that. Over time a tendency has manifested itself for two or three or four of the Twelve to dominate the others, either by straightforward means such as kinship-alliance, or by secret guile or the threat of force." That brooding look got darker. "We are not at our best, as a people, when rule is concentrated in the hands of just a few . . . and just one would be far worse. The memory of Vriha t'Rehu, that bloody and terrible woman, the Ruling Queen as she called herself, is too much with us still. Close enough she came to destroying both our worlds."

Ael shuddered. "For our people, as regards government, safety lies in numbers . . . the more, the better. But at present, though the outer forms of a representative democracy, as you would call it, may yet remain, the reality is otherwise. Our Empire has become a tyranny. There have been times when luck or the Elements have sent us tyrants who were benevolent, as there were such times in your own world. But such times are rare, and this is not one of them. The Three who rule the Twelve, right now, are a force under whom *mnhei'sahe* as we used to understand it has become a scarcity, too precious either to spend on ourselves or to waste on our enemies. For them, expediency has become all. And the Empire, in their hands, has become a tool used not as originally intended, to feed its people and further their lives and aspirations, but to keep power concentrated as it is now, in the hands of those who have long possessed it, and prefer to keep it that way."

She took a long drink of her ale, then sat for a few moments turning and turning the cup around in her hands. "The Three have ascended relatively young to power, and delight in using it; indeed their use of it has molded all the doings of Federation and Empire, one with the other, for the last half decade. They it was who started to send our ships across the Neutral Zone, spending the lives of brave officers to test the peace which had held so long and which so irked them. Theirs was the force behind the vote of the Senate which stripped my sister-daughter of her ship and her title and her name, after you stole the cloaking device from her, and sent her into exile, the Elements only know where. They it was who, when I began to speak out openly against them, sent me away to the Outmarches on *Cuirass* for that tour of duty intended at the least to punish me, and at best to bring about my death. And they were the ones who, before they ascended to power, started the researches which terminated in the work done at Levaeri V; the ones who ordered *Intrepid* captured and all its Vulcan crew to be put to death for the sake of the power which chemical mastery of Vulcan mind-control and mind-reading disciplines would give them and their creatures on ch'Rihan and ch'Havran."

She fell silent a moment. Jim watched with some admiration for the coolness with which she spoke of these people who had tried to destroy her. His own frustration at how badly she had been treated by the Empire she served was severe enough. *Would I be able to be that levelheaded about them, I wonder? And will she be able to stay this way . . . ?* "If I am bitter against them in my own regard," Ael said, "perhaps you will agree I have reason. But all my trouble began with an attempt to see the Three moved out of power by working within our own system. That attempt, and those which followed it, failed. That being the case, I came to you—for as I said at the time, when one's friends are helpless to make a difference, one turns even to one's enemies; especially the honorable ones. But it has not been enough, Jim. The work we have done together, while useful, yet falls short of what will cure the illness of which Levaeri V was only the symptom. Now I must raise what forces will answer me when I call, and move against my own world and people: though they call me traitor for it, and burn my name while I am still living, and curse it when I am dead."

Ael bowed her head.

Jim sat and considered, for the details of his sealed orders were on his mind. There had been a time when his own ancestors had been involved in a revolution like this, and he was proud now of that involvement. But four centuries' distance and the settled verdict of history now lent an aspect of comfortable respectability to that old war. Seen up close, as contemporaries, coups were not such comfortable companions. *At this end of time it's easy to say, yes, I would have been a patriot, I would have helped! But hindsight inevitably contaminates the vision. And being involved in a coup at its beginning, helping to hold the match to the fuse . . . For that* was the kind of help Ael was seeking from him.

He looked out at the stars. *On the other hand . . . sealed orders aside, if you see an injustice, and don't move to right it when you have a chance, history won't forget that, either.*

Jim turned back to her. "All right," he said. "So let's assume that your supporting force materializes as scheduled, and you sweep into the Eisn system, fight your way down to the surfaces of both planets, against whatever odds, put a significant number of troops on the ground, and carry the day. Then what?"

She leaned back and gave him a droll look. "Why, then that very day we have the Three and their minions dragged in chains down the Avenue of Processions in Ra'tleihfi, and put to the sword; and then from the ranks of the Senate, where here and there some old praetorial blood yet remains, we cause the elevation of twelve new Praetors . . . and then we go to our noonmeal."

Jim snorted. "Yes," Ael said, "it would be rather less simple than that, and I make no doubt there will be complications that neither of us could foresee. But one must start somewhere. Right now the Praetorate is too united under the Three's domination, and the Senate is too divided, for them to bring about a change in the status quo by the normal method. A credible threat to the Empire—or at the very least to the power structure at the top of it, and the armed forces which support that structure—will give them reason to change their thinking: especially when I make my cause known, and when it becomes obvious that I have power to back it."

"It may also give them reason to unite," Jim said, "and try to crush you."

"If the forces brought against them are sufficiently strong," Ael said, "I do not look for that. And additionally . . ."

She got that brooding look again. "Things are shifting," Ael said. "Increasingly there are signs that people around the Empire, not just on ch'Rihan and ch'Havran where the government's grip is tightest, are beginning to recall times when honor meant something—when we were content with what we had; when our people's history, painful and tragic as it has sometimes been, was a part of us, and not something we had to forget, or get over." Ael's look grew fierce. "If I must lead a force against my own world to rouse my people to take back their heritage, the power rightfully theirs, the thing worth fighting for . . . then so be it. There are, it seems, many who will follow me. For one thing, news of Levaeri V got out, and many people could see for themselves what that technology would make of our worlds if widely used. For another thing, the outworlds in particular, the colony planets and client systems in those spaces which march with the Klingon side of the Empire, have been suffering terribly of late. They are not all unarmed; indeed some of our oldest and most honored families, the great old Ship-Clans descended from the generation-ship captains, pilots and engineers who brought us to the Two Worlds, are settled out there in force. Once they were proud, and their voices were great in the Empire. But in recent years the government has sought to reduce their power, either by oppressing them directly, or by ignoring them, refusing to support their worlds. And now they are growing weary of this treatment . . . and growing restive."

"Restiveness is useful as an indicator," Jim said, "and early indications are always nice. But what happens if you raise the banner . . . and no one falls in behind you?"

Ael lifted her eyes to his. "Then I go over the hill by

myself," she said, "and take the consequences. I have done it before. If I die in so doing . . ." She raised her eyebrows. "Is it so bad a way to die? Even if no one answers the call to arms, if all the Empire from Eisn outward ignores me, and I must go down into ch'Rihan's gravity well alone . . . then alone I shall go."

The two of them sat quiet for some moments. Around them and behind them the lights of the rec deck were dimming as it slipped into gamma-shift mode, ship's night. The stars outside did not move, but hung there, still as watching eyes.

Then, very softly, Jim said:

"Like hell you will."

It was late again in Eveh tr'Anierh's study, and he had taken a moment away from the desk to try to stabilize some of the least stable of the piles of books on one of the shelves. With his arms full of books, he paused for a moment as he heard the front door open. *Now at this hour,* he thought, *who—*

He knew within two guesses. Not many people dare to come uninvited to a praetor's house after couch-time but another praetor; and of the other eleven of those—

The study door swung open. There was Urellh, and behind him, there was also poor Firh the dooropener, scandalized because he had been unable to stop this guest from interrupting his master, and terrified because of who the guest was. "Urellh," said tr'Anierh immediately, "come in; make yourself welcome. Firh, why are you yet up so late? Where is Serinn?" He was the night door-opener.

"He was away, Lord——"

"Well, no matter. To your couch, man: we have an early day tomorrow, you and I."

Firh bowed and closed the door, looking vaguely relieved. Urellh had already seated himself in the chair opposite the one which tr'Anierh had left pulled out. He was already pouring himself herbdraft from the pitcher waiting there on the tray, and the spicy scent of it wafted to tr'Anierh's nostrils as he turned his back on Urellh and went back to restacking the books on the shelves. "Well," he said, "you did not come here just to drink my draft, however fine the imported herbs might be."

"You have been too busy in your little glade of knowledge here, then," Urellh said, "to see the news tonight."

"I saw the sunset news," tr'Anierh said. "Once a day is enough for me. We normally get what else we need to see in session during the day. Or plenty enough of it for me, at any rate. What's amiss?"

"Ch'Havran," Urellh said, and said it as a curse. "The damned insurrectionists are out in the streets. Who would have thought they would have dared, so soon after the lesson they were taught three months ago? Or that we thought they had been taught. And whose damned name do you think they were shouting?"

Tr'Anierh could guess this, too, within a half a

guess; but he said nothing for the moment, finishing with one stack of books and beginning to dismantle the next. Outside the windows in one of the trees, a *dalwhin* tried a single piping note, then another, with the uncertainty of summer, when nesting was done and the immediacy had gone out of the defense of its territory. "If it is who I think," tr'Anierh said, "what matter? She is light-years away, soon to be a prisoner . . . or dead in battle."

"Oh indeed," Urellh said, "so you think, do you." He drank his cup of draft and slammed the cup down on the inlaid table. "What I want to know is what the news service thinks it's playing at, showing such things at all. If they'd just let well enough alone, such little local ructions would pass off without comment. But no, both worlds have to see it, and half the Empire, in a day or three. Out there where there's no control anymore, such ideas start to achieve common currency—"

"Which ideas?"

"Aah, the usual idiocy about our high history and how we've squandered it, and how our honor is in shreds and our Empire's wealth all bought with treachery—" He snorted. "Take the bread and the meat off their plates and the ale from their cups, and we'd see how soon they'd care a scrap for honor. But her name always gets worked into it somehow. As if any of them would shed a drop of green for her if it came to fighting." His look was sour. "Before this they did not dare put their heads up over the wall, for fear the Intelligence services would deal with them. And their agendas were always so different, anyway, that their own divisions and squabbling did for us what the Intelligence people failed to do. But now all of a sudden they've found a new name to cry. I wouldn't have thought them capable."

The *dalwhin* outside sang a long sweet phrase, about a breath's worth, in a minor key, then fell silent. Tr'Anierh raised his eyebrows at Urellh. "You know as well as I do," he said, "that the harder you try to keep these little groups' demonstrations from happening, the more attention they draw. Ignore them and they do pass off, eventually. People's memories are short. And as for the news services—" He shrugged, turned away from the shelf. "Let such things be shown commonly, and soon people stop paying attention to them; they become background noise."

Urellh did not answer him immediately. "There has been more news than only that," Urellh said after a few moments, softly. "Not on the news services: but it has been coming through, this past halfmonth, anyway. Ainleith. Mahalast. Orinwen. Taish. Relhinder." Tr'Anierh raised his eyebrows. They were all colony worlds of the so-called second class, worlds founded directly on emigration from the Two Worlds instead of by "second intention": not conquered client worlds, or "overspill" colonies of colonies.

"There have been demonstrations there as well," Urellh said. "All very proper, very polite. Petitions

153

passed in to the local governments, with thousands of names." He paused for a few long moments. "Treason," he said.

"For what do these petitions ask?" tr'Anierh said, though he knew.

"Treason," Urellh said again. "'Freedom.'" It was a growl. "Why, what else have we given them all these years but freedom to be safe, to be provided for, to have safe trade with the Hearthworlds and defense against those whom we know to be their enemies. Now let there be a slight change in policy, strictly temporary of course, but necessary, and you see quickly enough where their loyalties lie——" He broke off. "Damned Ship-Clan families," Urellh said softly, after a pause. "They have never really been one with us, not when we were in the Ships, and not afterward when our people came down out of the wretched things to live on real worlds again. There is no getting the steel out of their blood, or the vacuum out of their brains. Their time is done, you would think they would have the sense to see it by now. The Ships are fallen, the computers are dust, their time as the great 'guardians of our destiny' is over! But no, they cling to this 'nobility' that no one can see but them. History, heritage . . ." He snorted. "Anachronism! Time to look forward now, not back. The future is waiting for us, and all they can think of is division and backsliding when we should be united, looking to the future——"

"I would think," said tr'Anierh carefully, glancing

over at the table where Urellh had slammed his cup down and then reaching for a dusting cloth from the bottom shelf of one of the bookshelves, "that they too are a passing force, nearly spent. There are few enough of those old families left anymore. And were they ever so numerous, the thing that gave them their power base is now gone. Without the great Ships, what are they?"

Once again Urellh was silent for some moments. As tr'Anierh came around toward his desk, pausing by the table to mop up the spilled herbdraft, the other praetor looked up at tr'Anierh from under those dark eyebrows of his. In the subdued lighting of the room, tr'Anierh was suddenly stricken by how very dark and fierce the man looked.

"Everything is a light thing to you, is it not?" Urellh said. "At least, when one asks you about it to your face."

Tr'Anierh was opening his mouth to answer, but Urellh did not wait for him. "You have tried to forestall me," Urellh whispered: and the whisper was very cold. *"Why did you try to forestall me?"*

Tr'Anierh flushed first hot, then cold, and prayed that in this lighting, neither of them showed. For the moment he concentrated on folding up the dusting cloth.

"You have no taste for war," said Urellh. *"That is* your problem. Do you not see, are you too stupid to see, that our people do have one, if you do not? . . . and if you do *not* give them a war, every now and then, they will have one in your despite? You may play the fool with your own hide, tr'Anierh, and those of your creatures in Fleet that see fit to obey your orders. But not with *my* hide, and not with the lives of the people I rule."

The turn of phrase was one that tr'Anierh filed away carefully for future study . . . but right now he had little time to waste on it. "Our people," he said, putting the cloth aside, "would be better served if all this were finished quickly, rather than dragged out into war over one woman—"

"It is not merely over one woman! There is much more at stake, and the act was idiocy! Now we will go to this meeting, and the cursed Federation will say, 'Why should we believe anything you say? Here we have evidence of you crossing the Zone illegally after the woman and attacking her in our space.' Besides losing us seven ships—*seven ships!*—you have forfeited the moral high ground to the Federation! What can you have been thinking of?"

Tr'Anierh swallowed. In the quiet, the *dalwhin* in the tree outside sang another timid little phrase, a few piped notes, and fell silent again. "Rogue elements can easily enough be blamed," he said. "The Federation know as well as we do that there are divisions among our people, Urellh. They have as many spies among us as we have among them; do you think I do not know?"

"I know that your heart is going cold in your side," said Urellh, "and I don't intend to permit that to ruin our plans. You are growing too like the indecisive ones in the Senate: you put out your hand to the sword and then snatch it back when you smell the blood on the blade." His eyes narrowed. "There are some, even in the Praetorate, who so fear a just war that they would even leak information to the enemy to prevent it. Just how," Urellh said, much more softly, "did the Federation get word about the mind-control project, for example? And do not tell me the despicable t'Rllailieu told them. She got that information from somewhere. And it would not have been from one of the sottish wind-talkers in the Senate; the information was not disseminated that widely. It would have been from among the Twelve, from one of the very *Praetorate*, tr'Anierh! Some one of us, maybe even more than one of us, is a traitor."

He looked long and hard at tr'Anierh. "You will not lay that at *my* House's gate, Urellh," said tr'Anierh, as steadily as he could. "And certainly not publicly; not unless you wish to find out exactly how quickly I 'snatch my hand back' when accused with such a calumny, and how 'lightly' I take everything. I would not trouble to take the matter to the judiciars. I would have you meet me in the Park."

Urellh's face stilled a little at that. "And as for this latest matter," said tr'Anierh, "if I knew of it, what of it? If it had succeeded, the Sword would either be safely destroyed, forever out of the hands of our enemies, or else it would now be on the way back to where it belongs. Our people's pride would to a great extent have been restored, and we would not now need to put our head into the *thra'i*'s mouth to find out whether it has any teeth left or not. Has it ever occurred to you that it might have grown new ones faster than the old ones were pulled, and might bite indeed? What if the Federation suspects the diplomatic mission for exactly what it is, the prelude to war, and decides to strike first? —And on the other hand, our own sources in Starfleet tell us how divided that organization has been of late. Very nearly they did not agree to meet the mission at all. What would we have done then? We would have been left with no t'Rllaillieu, no Sword, and no recourse except to invade in the routine manner, with the result being a full mobilization on Starfleet's side instead of the partial, uncertain, halfhearted one we see now. The Klingons would fall on our outworlds in force, in numbers, without a second thought. It is we who would be forced into a two-front war, not they. And what remained of the Empire after that—after the Klingons' brutality and the Federation's cruel mercy—would be a pitiful thing indeed, not worthy of the name. You are to count yourself most fortunate that they accepted, and that matters stand even now as well as they do."

Another brief silence: but the *dahwhin* outside sang no more. "You said nothing of these misgivings before we stood up before the Senate and proposed the mission," Urellh said. "I question whether they are not rather recently assumed . . . possibly in the wake of the failure of this 'rogue element.' The actions of which are themselves an act of war, in contravention of the Treaty—so that any protection we might have had from that tattered rag of a document is lost to us now. I think it only right that *your* creatures in the diplomatic mission should be allowed to assume the responsibility for explaining it to the Federation negotiators. You are to count yourself fortunate that the fools will most likely accept the explanation, since they know so little of what passes among our worlds . . . the Elements be praised. Equally it will be fortunate for you, in the long run, that they know nothing of the 'package' which will soon be on its way to them; for this nasty little business has at last decided *that* destination. That only will save your skin, when all the reckoning is done after the battle is complete. And meanwhile—" He got up, walked around the table, and put his face quite close to tr'Anierh's, nearly close enough to be an insult—though not quite. "It was an act of the most utter folly, meant to make me look a fool," said Urellh, "and I will not forget it."

He stormed out, and slammed the door behind him.

Tr'Anierh stood there until he heard the outer door close again. Then he breathed out a long breath, and went back over to the bookshelf and chose another pile of bound codices to reorganize.

Honor, tr'Anierh thought. Urellh had not said *mnhei'sahe;* he had used the lesser word, *omien.* Tr'Anierh considered that. It came to him that very few people seemed to say *mnhei'sahe* anymore. It was as if the word hurt them somehow. Even he himself avoided using it; perhaps not to be seen distinguishing himself too obviously from others, as one championing virtue—that was a sure way to cause your enemies to go tunneling like *llhei* for proof that your virtue was a sham.

But then the word always did have edges. And held incorrectly . . . it cuts. . . .

He started making, in his mind, a list of the people he would need to call in the morning. Urellh was a bad and sore-tempered enemy when he had been crossed. Sometimes these moods passed off him quickly: sometimes they did not do so at all, or took long months to abate. At the moment, that could be a problem. Tr'Anierh thought about what to do . . .

. . . and about the seven ships.

Jim sat up in one of the briefing rooms for a long while, late that night, after leaving the rec deck and seeing Ael down to the transporters and back to *Bloodwing*. He was looking at the maps of the Federation, the Klingon Empire, and the Romulan Empire, and he was thinking hard.

The room was one of those with a big holographic display in the middle of the table. There Jim had sketched out for himself in the display, in red, a five-parsec sphere around the spot where the Rihannsu were scheduled to cross the border tomorrow. The larger portion of the task force which had been sent to do escort duty would meet them there and bring them into Federation space, to the spot selected for the rendezvous. Then the extra ships would depart, leaving the numbers equal at the rendezvous point: and talks would begin.

Jim looked at that red sphere now and thought: *Why here?* The Romulans had specified where they intended to cross the Zone for these talks. The Federation had made no counteroffer.

And why not? Jim thought. That by itself struck him as a failure. *Your opponent wants to do something—you force him to do something else. Partly to see how he reacts. Partly to make sure you stay in control of the game.* But for some reason, Starfleet had not reacted to that particular move. It was as if they had conceded something early, something they didn't see as particularly valuable, in a larger strategy.

For his own part, Jim had played too much chess with Spock—2D, 3D, and 4D—to much like the idea of conceding moves to anyone, especially first moves. They were strategically as important to him as later ones. And any move that did not advance your game, push you into your opponent's territory and threaten him somehow, was a wasted move. Wasting moves was criminal.

There was nothing terribly interesting about this part of space. It was largely barren. *But a lot of Triangulum space is like that*, Jim thought, *until you get in further.* There were richer spaces, better provided with planets with suns, and developed planets at that, in the Aries direction. But that whole area was also much better provided with Federation infrastructure. There were two starbases there, 18 at Hamal and 20 at gamma Arietis / Mesarthim; each was well provided with weaponry of its own and a large complement of starships, and Starbase 20 and its starship complement had the additional advantage of being staffed by the Mesarth, probably one of the most aggressive species in the Federation ("except for humans," Spock had once commented rather ruefully). *If I were a Romulan,* Jim thought, *I wouldn't waste my time going that way. Too much resistance. . . .*

But it still left him with the question: Why *here?*

Jim looked at the map for a while more. Leaving aside the issue of the "diplomatic mission," which he thought was as likely to be the spearhead of an invasion force as anything else, Jim was also thinking about the seven ships that *Enterprise* and *Bloodwing* had met at 15 Trianguli. *Someone was willing to take the chance of throwing away seven capital ships,* he thought, *for something. And not just for* Ael. Redoubtable as her reputation was, seven ships just for *Bloodwing* made no sense. They were even too much for *Bloodwing* and *Enterprise* together.

Someone wanted to test our preparedness, he thought. *If they got her, too . . . fine. But something else is going on. They wanted to test this area, not just the area over by the rendezvous point.*

Jim leaned his chin on his fist and looked at the

hologram, telling it to rotate so that he could see the way the Klingon and Romulan empires interpenetrated one another. The only "regular" boundary in the area was the Neutral Zone, which was a one-light-year-thick section of an ovoid "shell" with Federation space on one side and Romulan space on the other. Elsewhere, bumps and warts of Klingon and Romulan territory stuck into and out of the main volumes of the two Empires with great irregularity where they bounded one another. The contact surfaces suggested many years of the two players playing put-and-take in that part of space.

Jim stopped the hologram and instructed the viewing program to zoom in on the Neutral Zone. As he did, the monitoring satellites became visible, scattered fairly evenly along and across the Zone's curvature. *Now, were those ships detected coming across the Zone?* Jim thought. *And if not, why not? What's the matter with the monitoring satellites and stations?*

Is it possible one or more of them have been knocked out, or sabotaged? By whom? And why wouldn't we have heard?

He pulled his padd over and made a note on it, one of many he had made while studying the map. *And if the ships were detected crossing,* he thought, *why weren't we alerted by Starfleet?*

Jim tossed the stylus to the table and looked at the map again. The satellites were much on his mind. *If we have here some program of sabotage which has*

163

been in preparation for a while and is now ready to be tested . . . was this possibly the first test?

If it was . . . what will their reaction be when their seven ships don't come home again?

He kept looking at the map. Could it be that what we're looking at here, Jim thought, is an intended breakout in two different places? One in the area where the "diplomatic mission" will be—and one over here by 15 Tri? It will, after all, have the "New Battle" cachet. . . . One of his Strat-Tac instructors, years ago, had mentioned to him some strategists' tendency to overlook a possible location for conflict because there had just been one there, the idea apparently being that an enemy was as unlikely to immediately fight twice on the same battlefield as lighting was to strike twice. This was, of course, a fallacy: a smart enemy, if he had the resources to waste and the brains to pull it off, might stage an unsuccessful battle on likely ground in order to tempt an unwary adversary onto it for a second and more murderous passage at arms. You'd have to wonder why they were bothering with this one spot, though, Jim thought. Either because they've been assembling matériel close to it, or because it's convenient to something else.

The Klingons, maybe? 15 Tri was convenient enough to the area where the Neutral Zone, the Klingon Empire, and the un-Zoned part of the Romulan Empire drew close together. A lot of scope for confusion there, Jim thought. Suppose the Romulans break out there—and instead of coming for us, swing around and attack the Klingons from our direction. Then duck back into the Zone in the confusion of the war that's already going on elsewhere, near the rendezvous point, say, and maybe somewhere else along the Zone as well.

The hair stood up on the back of Jim's neck. *Two-front war,* he thought. *Bad. Very bad.*

. . . So that's one possibility, he thought, sitting back in his chair. *And there's another. One of these two breakouts is a feint, to distract us from something more important happening somewhere else.*

He sat looking up at the map. *You must assume that they are preparing some great stroke against you,* Ael had said. *Revenge . . .*

And they'll have more reason for it than ever, now, Jim thought. *Seven more of their ships, we've written off . . . with their own weapon, too.* He touched the tabletop and started the map rotating again, more slowly this time. *I need information we probably aren't going to be able to get,* he thought. *I need to know what Rihannsu resources are sited over here at the moment.* He looked over at the area where the two Empires ran together near the Neutral Zone. *And what's been moved into that area recently . . .*

Again, information he probably wasn't going to get: certainly not over an open channel from Starfleet. Not that he didn't want to talk to them anyway about the status of the monitoring satellites, and those seven ships.

Those ships....

The idea that there should be a leak to the Ri-hannsu from Starfleet upset him profoundly. But at the same time, such leaks could be used to the advantage of a commander in the field . . . if you fed the correct information into them. You might be able to track the leak by where the information came out, in what shape. And even if you couldn't, your opponent would be misled . . . with results that you could turn to your own advantage.

Jim sat there a long while. *Ael will be back in the morning*, he thought, *to look in on that conference with Scotty and K's't'lk. This is the last chance we're going to have to confab before we have half of Starfleet looking over our shoulders.*

Time to make our plans....

"Jim," said McCoy's voice behind him.

"I thought you'd turned in," Jim said.

"No," McCoy said. "Just off having a talk with Spock."

Jim raised his eyebrows. "Anything I need to know abour?"

"Ael!"

"What else," Jim said, and yawned, and rubbed his eyes.

McCoy came to sit down by him, and looked up at the map. "Yes," he said. "I thought so."

"And what's your tactical assessment, Doctor?"

"That you're about to head straight up the creek without a paddle."

Jim would have phrased it a little more strongly. "Bones," he said, "thank you. I'll call the Strat-Tac department at Starfleet and tell them you said so."

McCoy's look was unusually gentle. "Jim, listen to me. The way you're heading, you are shortly going to be caught in between *Bloodwing* and Starfleet again. It's not like you to make the same mistake twice."

"Well," Jim said, "you can put your mind at rest on that account, Bones, because this time I wasn't the one who made it." He looked up at the map. *"They* did."

"Starfleet?"

"They did not send *Enterprise* to meet *Bloodwing* here just because they know she and I are . . ." He was about to say "friends," but the word suddenly seemed both likely to be completely misunderstood, even by Bones, and completely inaccurate, for reasons he could barely describe to himself. He looked up to find McCoy looking closely at him. "Associates," Jim said.

"And in some ways," Bones said, "very much alike."

"That may be so," Jim said. "But they expect me to find out what she's going to do—or worse still, to anticipate it—and to act on what I discover, in Starfleet's best interests."

"And can you do that?" McCoy said.

"It's not a 'can,'" Jim said, "as you know very well. It's a 'must.' My oaths to Starfleet are intact, Bones, and I intend to keep them that way."

"But at the same time . . ."

"She has her own priorities, Bones," Jim said, settling back in the chair. "She wants peace . . . but she knows the only way that's going to happen, on the Romulan side of things, is war: and sooner, rather than later." He was quiet for a few moments. "I'm short of less slanted data at the moment, and I'd welcome some. But right now there isn't any."

"There may be some," McCoy said, "when the Romulans arrive."

Jim raised his eyebrows at that. "Oh?"

"Just a guess," McCoy said, "but I would be very surprised if at least one of the sources Starfleet's been gettin' its data from was not on that mission when it turns up."

Jim eyed McCoy thoughtfully. "Medicine is a creative art," Bones said, "just like command . . . and doctors get hunches the same way starship captains do."

"I hope you're right," Jim said. "Anyway . . ." He looked up at the map again. "Ael is a realist, if nothing else. I think she knows as well as I do that the situation, as it's presently shaping up, will result in war, no matter what she does. Equally from the realist's point of view, she has decided to play the active role, not the passive; to take control of the forces which are looking toward her now, as a catalyst, and to use them."

Jim slumped in the chair and rubbed his eyes again. "Yup. She's a catalyst, all right," he said. "*Nuhirrien* . . ." McCoy, very softly.

"Wha?"

"You said people there were looking toward her. That's *nuhirrien*, almost literally," Bones said. "It's Rihannsu. Charisma, we would say . . . the quality of attracting people, of being followed by them." He let out a long breath.

"I keep forgetting, you did that chemical-learning course for the language."

"Sometimes I still wish I hadn't. I can't even *look* at a bowl of soup anymore."

Jim thought about that, and resolved firmly not to ask why. "Anyway," Bones said, *"nuhirrien* is a dangerous characteristic, for Rihannsu. Dangerous for Ael, too, if it seems she's got it."

"Why?"

"It's more associational than anything else," McCoy said. "The Ruling Queen had *nuhirrien*, they say. People would follow her, the way they once followed Hitler, centuries ago."

"Into tremendous evil," Jim said softly.

"Sometimes. It can blind people to the realities."

"We'd better hope it doesn't come to that," he said. "Bones, was there anything else? I'm about done here."

"Just so you know," McCoy said, "that, despite the imponderables . . . we're with you."

Jim stood up. "It's worth knowing," he said.

He killed the display and made for the door, with McCoy in tow. "You know," Jim said, "you're the one who should be talking to her. You've got the language, now."

"She's been avoiding me," McCoy said as they went down the corridor, "or so it seems."

There was data, and a piece that Jim wasn't sure what to do with. "Well," he said, "see what you can do about it. Choices are going to have to be made thick and fast around here in a couple of days, and I don't have all the information I need as yet."

"I'll do what I can," Bones said as Jim paused outside the turbolift, and its doors opened for him. "Meanwhile, you should get some sleep. Early meeting in the morning."

"Yes. Good night, Bones."

"Night, Jim," McCoy said, and the turbolift doors shut on him.

"Deck twelve," Jim said. The lift hummed upward.

The big end of a court-martial, Jim thought, and shivered.

Chapter Five

IF THERE was one thing Arrhae had not been expecting about going to space, it was having very much room to do it in. Long long ago, in another life (or so it felt), she had been used to fairly cramped quarters on starships; not unpleasantly so, but you wouldn't have room in your quarters for a game of *nha'rei*, either. Since then, in all her life as *hru'hfe* in House Khellian, the sense of her personal life as something lived in a fairly tight, small space had been reinforced to the point where she simply forgot about the possibility of things being any other way. On becoming senator, and more senior in House Khellian than any servant, things had changed . . . though again, not to extremes: the house was richer in honor than in space.

But once again everything had shifted. She had climbed into the flitter that had been sent for her the evening after she talked to Eveh tr'Anierh—having spent the whole day, it seemed to her, not packing, but reassuring the household that she would be all right—and realized that her life had become peculiar again.

The flitter had not taken her to the spaceport, but straight up and out of atmosphere, to the new heavy cruiser *Gorget*. She had stepped from the comfort of the flitter out onto a great shining floor in the cruiser's shuttle bay, with yet another honor guard waiting, this time of Fleet personnel; and these had brought small arms up to honor poise and walked her through the corridors of *Gorget*, Arrhae thought, like a queen. At a door high up in the deck structure of the cruiser they had halted, and one had opened the door for her; and Arrhae had walked into a space in which she could have had that *nha'rei* game, if she had chosen.

Huge windows on space, and carpeting, and antique furniture, and artwork, and a table off to one side, laden with food, and looking so good that Arrhae had to remind herself to treat it with disdain at the moment—the place was palatial. *If all Fleet lived like this, I could see why young Rihannsu would fight for commissions,* Arrhae thought. But she had a strong feeling that most crewmen didn't live like this; she knew that *Gorget* had recently been refitted, probably with an eye to the transport of notables and government figures. *If a small fish like me gets rooms like these,* she wondered, *what do the more senior senators and the diplomats get?*

The honor guard had presently taken itself away, and Arrhae had discovered that the suite came with a small service staff of its own—maidservant and steward, the more senior of whom, Ffairrl the steward, bowed and scraped to Arrhae in a most unseemly way, one that suggested that he was either a spy (possible) or used to being mistreated by the high-ranking guests (equally possible). She allowed him to show her around the suite—a master bedroom with a bath suite that must have been most extravagant in water use, even aboard a starship where water could be manufactured at will from ramscoop "scrapings"; a bedroom and sitting room which together were nearly a quarter the size of House Khellian's Great Hall; and the outer meeting room and sitting room, with a buffet sideboard loaded with piles of food and pitchers of drink, and a small ancillary workroom and study, equipped with a state-of-the-art computer and communications suite. The tour over, Ffairrl begged to be allowed to give Arrhae food and drink. This she allowed him to do, and then sent him away, over his protests, while she wandered through the place, getting the feel of it and wondering where the listening and scanning devices were.

In the little office Arrhae had found a tidy printout of information concerning the mission. This went well enough with the "solid" information which she had received by courier that morning, and had read between fits of dealing with her own pan-icky household staff. The solid had contained copies of the legislation that had empowered the mission to leave, the mission statement, the document with which the mission would present the Federation on arrival, and a much fatter document containing speculation by Intel staff on the Federation's possi-ble reactions to the presentation document. The printout sitting on the desk included names and some limited personal information on each of the Rihannsu delegates empowered to actually negoti-ate on the Empire's behalf, the senators assisting them, and the so-called observer group, of which Arrhae was one. She flipped along to her own description and was amused to see its brev-ity. *Signed 20.10.02156*, it said. *Senator for i'Ramnau-Hwaimmen. House: Khellian. Decora-tions: none.* Many of the other biographies had a category that said "Service," but not hers. Arrhae wondered if someone had been embarrassed by the prospect of the jokes it might enable.

She had looked up from her examination of her biography that evening at the slight shudder that had gone through the ship. *Gorget* was moving out on impulse, heading past the golden glare of Eisn; when there was enough distance between her and the star, she went into warp. Arrhae had breathed out when that happened, and then realized how she had been holding her breath. *Anything could happen to me now,* she had thought. *What if I never see that star again? . . .*

The thought had left her peculiarly cold. Arrhae had pushed it aside, taking her reading out into the main room, where she could keep the buffet sideboard company.

The next day, and the day after that and the day after that, she had been kept busy with meetings with the other delegates, other members of the Observing Group, and with more reading. Arrhae knew that she had very much been tossed in at the deep end of Rihannsu politics, but she was moderately well prepared for that: her years on ch'Rihan had not been spent only telling people where to dust and mop. Part of the job Starfleet had assigned her was to be as perfect in understanding of the language as she could, and this had meant doing all the listening and reading, of all kinds, for which her position allowed her time. By virtue of that—time stolen late at night, reading and watching the news services, days spent in judicious eavesdropping—she had learned as much about the politics of the Two Worlds as most Rihannsu ever did, and more than many ever bothered to. Now, of course, the game had moved up to a higher level, and she started meeting the faces who belonged to names which until now she had only read or heard of.

Noonmeal on the first day had been another lavishly catered affair—Arrhae made a note to herself to find out whether the ship had a gymnasium, or even a steambath where she might try to melt some of the carbohydrates off her between "briefings." It had ostensibly been informal, a "meet and greet" gathering of the delegates, negotiators, and observers. The way people carried themselves, and the groups into which they gathered, soon enough told Arrhae that, despite the polite introductions, everyone knew what everyone else's job was, and what their status was, and anyone who stepped out of position would soon enough be reminded. The negotiators kept to themselves, talking in a jovial and important way, and looked down on the delegates: the delegates did the same and looked down on the observers. The observers, having no one to look down on but the officers and staff of *Gorget*, did so, and Arrhae watched with considerable annoyance as they ordered the poor underlings around.

Arrhae for her own part tried to be social with her fellow observers as she met them over the second and third days. They were mostly jurists and tribunes—sober, sometimes somber people who seemed rather taken aback by the position into which they had suddenly been elevated—and a couple of other senators whom Arrhae knew slightly. One of these, a round, blunt, balding little man named Imin tr'Phalltei, had plainly expected her to carry the drinks tray around out of habit when he met her first in the Senate, and was openly surprised to see her here. The other, a handsome, tall, broadshouldered woman named Odirne t'Melanth, a Havraunsu with a name like that, had greeted her kindly when they met at that noonmeal, and Arrhae had realized that she found all this as disconcerting, and as absurd, as Arrhae did. "That lot over there," Odirne said, signing with her chin at the negotiating group which had ostentatiously seated itself, as if of right, up at the top of the table, "do they even want to breathe the same air as we do? Great swaths of observing we'll be able to do, indeed, once they get down to their work. As if they'll let us near them when they're making their alleged minds up about what to do!"

At first glimpse Arrhae was inclined to agree with her. Some of the negotiators were not exactly congenial types. And two of them were praetors, though not on the level of the Three, of course—none of the Triumvirate would go out on a mission like this: their job was to sit home and rule on the information the underlings, even the very high-class underlings, sent to them. One of the two praetors wore a face Arrhae recognized slightly from McCoy's trial: Hloal t'Illialhlae, the tall, dark, hawk-faced woman who had been wife to the commander of *Battlequeen*, one of the ships lost to the Federation attack on Levaeri V. His death had made a martyr of him, and a harpy of her—if anyone would be pushing for the last drop of blood from the Federation in this negotiation, it would be she. The other praetor was Gurrhim tr'Siedhri, a great name on ch'Havran. He was a big, bluff, growling *mirhwen* of a man, a firebreathing warrior and former senator, one of the

stranger and more individual figures in the Praetorate, and very much a nobleman in the old mold—
as proud of being a farmer (if on a spectacular scale,
for his family's lands spread around a quarter of the
planet) as a poet. He was one of very few exceptions
to the rule that the negotiators and general delegates
on the mission were inimical to the Federation.
Tr'Siedhri did not like the Federation much, but he
did not hate it either; and he emphatically did not
fear it—which, Arrhae thought, was possibly a con-
tributing cause to his lack of hatred. Either way, his
presence here was something of a puzzle to Arrhae,
for he was ill liked by most of his other praetors,
who had to put up with him whether they liked it or
not because of the vast wealth and power his family
had amassed over the past three centuries. *Unless,*
Arrhae thought, *someone has sent him here to em-
barrass him somehow—which will happen if he tries
to treat the Federation fairly, and all the others side
against him.*

*Or possibly someone wants to try to get rid of
him,* said some small suspicious voice in the back of
Arrhae's head.

There might always be suspicion . . . but Rihannsu
life was full of unproven suspicion and paranoia, and
eventually it would fade.

Arrhae thought about that as the second and third
days went by, and she went to meetings and first-
meals and lastmeals with her fellow observers, making sure that she was available for the contacts she

had been told would come. The one that did come, finally, on the morning of the third day, was as unwelcome as it could have been.

Her steward was bustling around trying to feed her, and Arrhae had been trying to resist him, while attempting to put right the formal clothes that she had packed—they had all looked good in the clothespress, all these kilts and flowing dark tunics, but now they seemed to require endless belting and pinning to drape as they were meant to. And the doorchime had gone, and Arrhae had breathed out in annoyance; it would be the "door-opener"—not that *Gorget's* doors did not open automatically by themselves, but this particular Fleet officer was doing the same office as a ground-bound opener, arriving to escort guests around the corridors of the ship, which was all too easy to become lost in, and making sure they got where they were needed without putting their noses in anywhere they didn't belong, or stealing the silver. "Of your courtesy, get that," Arrhae had said to the steward, turning away to try to straighten out one more wayward pin, and then very carefully sitting down to her dinner. She was ravenous: the good dark smell of the *osilh* stew that Ffairrl had laid out on the little table beside the most comfortable chair had been making her stomach rumble, and Arrhae was determined to do something about that quickly, before she embarrassed herself in the day's first meeting.

The door slipped open and the steward said not a

word. Arrhae sighed, looked up . . . and found herself looking at Commander t'Radaik of the Rihannsu Intelligence Service.

What have I done to deserve this, Arrhae thought, trying to ignore the shiver that ran down her spine. The woman stood there, with those oblique eyes and sharp cheekbones of hers, tall and cool and good-looking in her dark, green-sashed uniform of tunic and breeches and too-shiny boots, and gazed down from her considerable height at Arrhae with an expression that suggested it took more than clothes and a signet to make the senator. Still, *"Deihu,"* she said, and bowed: and Arrhae gave about her two-thirds of a breath's bow from where she sat, not an overly committal gesture, one way or the other.

Arrhae looked over at the steward. "Our," she said, so that t'Radaik would be deprived of the opportunity to say it first. Ffairrl took himself away at speed.

"Well, *Deihu,"* said t'Radaik, looking around her with incompletely concealed amusement, "you seem to have settled in nicely."

"Except for interruptions," Arrhae said, "which not the Elements Themselves could prevent, it seems. What can I do for you, Commander?" She lifted the ale cup standing beside her plate, and drank.

T'Radaik bent that cool, arrogant regard on her again. "You have spoken in the past with the Terran, MakKhoi," she said.

"With no great pleasure," Arrhae said, and at the time it had been true. She picked up a small round flatbread that was still warm, tore it in two, and turned her attention to the plate of dark, spicy *osilh* stew which Ffairrl had laid out for her.

"You were . . . close to him." She was watching Arrhae very closely.

"Only in terms of seeing to his needs," Arrhae said, "as one might see to the needs of a guest of one's House." And irked by the intensity of t'Radaik's regard, she scooped up a little of the *osilh* with the flatbread, and ate. It was a calculated insult, to eat in front of someone and not offer them anything, especially if they fancied themselves your equal . . . but right now, Arrhae didn't care.

T'Radaik's eyes narrowed. "And he treated you in a friendly manner."

"In that he did not kill me when last we met," Arrhae said, becoming increasingly annoyed as she began to suspect where this was leading, "if you regard that as 'friendly': yes."

"You might then have reason to be grateful to him," said t'Radaik, "and to wish him well."

"I might also feel like killing him should we meet again," Arrhae said, tearing off another bit of bread and scooping up more stew with it, "but somehow I doubt that such an action would suit your intentions at the moment."

T'Radaik gave Arrhae a lofty look. "It would not. The Service requires your assistance. You will be given a package which will be——"

T'Radaik stopped suddenly as Arrhae put down

the piece of bread and fixed her with an angry stare. Arrhae lifted her right hand, turning its back to the Intelligence officer so that her signet was in plain view.

"The Service may indeed desire the *Deihu*'s assistance," Arrhae said, keeping her voice level, "but the Service is the *Senate*'s servant. Does it not say so, in great handsome letters, right around the seal emblazoned across your main building in Ra'tleihfi?"

T'Radaik simply looked at her. "I have been charged by the Praetor Eveh tr'Anierh to assist you," Arrhae said, "and to *his* wishes, I am obedient. But I would advise you to mend your manners, Commander, and mind your tone: or the praetor will hear of both. There is rarely such a galling sight, or one so likely to provoke the great to action, as an ill-behaved servant stepping out of its place."

T'Radaik opened her mouth. "And you are thinking that you knew me when I was only a *hru'hfe*," Arrhae said softly. "Think more quietly, Commander. Things change, in this world. 'Half the Elements are mutable; nothing stays the same,' the song says. And no matter what I was three months ago, the office of senator still commands some respect. Now tell me about this package, and whatever else you need me to know, and then begone: I have no intention of allowing you to make me late for my next meeting."

T'Radaik swallowed, a woman choking down anger, but not dismissing it: it would be saved carefully for another time. "The Service has a small package which it asks you to deliver," she said. "It will be left here in your rooms later today. Should the Terran MakKhoi be present at the negotiations, you are requested to see that it comes to him."

"Not without knowing what is in it," Arrhae said, picking up the rolled-up morsel of flatbread and popping it into her mouth.

T'Radaik frowned. "That is no affair of yours."

"Indeed it is," Arrhae said after a moment, "for a senator's *mnhei'sahe* rides on such knowledge, and on acting correctly upon it. I know enough of how the Service works to desire to be sure of what passes through my hands."

"A data chip," said t'Radaik. "Nothing more."

"Oh? Well, I shall open it first, and read every word."

Arrhae thought as she tore off one more bit of flatbread that taking on quite so assertive a shade of green did not improve t'Radaik's otherwise highbred looks. "I am not such a fool as to think it is love poetry," Arrhae said. "It will either be something that does us good, or does McCoy or the Federation some harm. I will know which before I assist you."

T'Radaik looked at her darkly. Then she said, "Disinformation."

Arrhae waited.

"There are Federation spies among us," t'Radaik said, "and you more than most people here should know it."

183

This stroke Arrhae had been expecting, and now she raised her eyebrows and gave t'Radaik an ironic look. The thought of what had happened to her old master Vaebn tr'Lhoell after he "sold" her away into the safety of House Khellian was much with Arrhae, but if t'Radaik expected her to react to the painful memory with terror, she had misjudged her. "Such is inevitable," Arrhae said: "as inevitable as our having spies in the Federation, I would suppose. So?" She used the bread to eat one last bit of stew.

"We catch them, sometimes," said t'Radaik, and this time she actually smiled. "Usually we manage to get at least some useful information out of them before we kill them. In this case, we managed to get quite a lot."

"I am delighted for you," Arrhae said. "Again: so?"

"We desire that the information the spy sought, along with other data of our own providing, should come to the Federation by quicker means than usual," t'Radaik said. "Seeing that you have had contact with the criminal and spy MakKhoi in the recent past, you are the perfect one to pass it to him. If you must justify your actions, you will pretend concern for him, and feign that this information comes from someone who was trying to contact him when he was on ch'Rihan last—for we have learned that his capture by our forces was not an accident. It was planned by the Federation itself, to allow him to check on some of their agents here."

Arrhae allowed herself to look astonished while she took another drink of ale, relishing the burning fruit of it as much as t'Radaik's annoyed look. "They must have little concern whether he lives or dies," she said.

"Little enough, though they make such a great noise about his value as a starship officer. But there are indications that some in Starfleet are becoming weary of *Enterprise*'s officers in general, not just her captain, and wish they could be rid of them." T'Radaik smiled. "Possibly the only goal we share. McCoy's being sent on this mission of espionage may have been a way to reduce the number of those officers by one. In any case, at least one of the Federation spies on ch'Rihan was instructed to try to make contact with McCoy while he was here, passing him certain information about the Empire. He failed to make that contact. But he also failed to sufficiently cover the tracks of his attempt to make it. We caught him, and he gave us the information he had been preparing for MakKhoi. Now, having examined it, we desire the data to reach MakKhoi . . . suitably altered. That information will come by him to *Bloodwing* . . . and once there, will do its best work." Her smile was that of a woman enjoying this prospect entirely too much.

"For all this trouble," Arrhae said, "I hope you may be sure of that."

"Oh, we will be informed promptly enough when the information has come where it needs to be."

Will you really. "Well," Arrhae said, trying to sound offhanded about it as she put down the cup, "this sounds as if it will not unduly affect my honor.

I will find a way to pass the chip to MakKhoi, should he present himself."

"We are sure he will," t'Radaik said. "The first night of the meeting with the Federation starships, to-morrow night, there will be a social occasion——" Her look was sardonic. "As if one can be social with such vile creatures, half aliens, half animals. Nonetheless, we will go along with the charade, and at this meeting you will certainly have the opportunity to speak with MakKhoi, and to pass him the material in question."

A soft chime came from the office: the alarm which Arrhae had set in her computer. She reached for the lap-cloth by her plate, dusted her hands with it, and stood up. "Very well," she said, and very rudely turned her back on t'Radaik, going off to fetch her carryall for the meeting she was about to attend.

"See to the package's delivery, then. You may go."

The door hissed open. Arrhae turned and just caught sight of t'Radaik's back going out. As the door closed again, Arrhae permitted herself just the slightest smile. She detested that woman, and she suspected t'Radaik had known as much before Ar-rhae ever opened her mouth. *No harm in letting her know she is right*, Arrhae thought.

At least, she hoped there would be none. . . .

It was summer in that hemisphere of Sammethe, and the weather had been holding fair for some while: hot and sunny, the sky piled high with good-weather cloud. In and out of that cloud, the rakish and deadly shapes of Grand Fleet shuttles could be seen all day, ferrying troops and equipment up to the birds-of-prey, the great starships presently in orbit. Now it was sunset, the heat of the day cooling. Mijne t'Ethien leaned against the fiberplas surface next to the door of the group shelter where she and fifty others, men and women, slept together since the government warnings of imminent attack had gone out, and the ingathering to the secure site at the planet's main spaceport, Tharawe. The hum of the place that one heard all day, from the habitués of the other five thousand houses of fifty, always began to hush down as dusk crept in. Now, in that peace, with her washing done and the daymeal inside her, Mijne leaned there and looked past the security fence toward the spaceport field, and was filled with wonder. Early that morning the sky had been full of the ugly swooping shapes of Klingon vessels, of phaserfire and the shriek of impulse engines. Now it was empty and peaceful again, and only the occasional shuttle going about its business broke the silence.

"They beat them," Mijne said to herself. "It is a miracle."

Behind her, a rough old voice said, "It is the dawn of a disaster; one which will start tomorrow."

Mijne turned to look at her grandfather with a mixture of annoyance and fondness. He had been predicting disasters since the two of them had been brought here. "Resettlement," the government had called it, "due to a state of emergency". "Internment," Amyn tr'Ethien had muttered when the message came down the terminal on that rainy morning, "as a matter of expediency."

"Don't be silly, Grandsire," Mijne had said then: and she said it again now. She had been annoyed at having to shut up the summerhouse just after it had been opened, but it seemed foolish to rail against the government's attempts to keep them all safe, and there was no protecting a population scattered as thinly across a planet as Sammethe's was. The growing Grand Fleet presence stationed at the planet would have had to fly all over the place, patrolling living area and wasting its resources and manpower. It made much more sense to gather them all together where some security could be found. "The Klingons, it seems, hit our defenses as hard as they could, and couldn't break through except to destroy a few hangars and small ships on the ground, not even anything important."

"You believe that, do you," her grandsire said. Mijne rolled her eyes. She did not mind being the last member of her family alive to take care of him: one had, after all, a duty to one's House. But he could be annoying sometimes, and since they came here he had embarrassed Mijne with his outspoken opinions and his doomsaying a goodly number of times.

"Why shouldn't I believe it?" Mijne said, walking away from the common house.

He walked away with her, linking his arm through hers, plainly knowing her intention—to get him away from there before he embarrassed her further in front of those with whom they were currently rooming—and clearly amused by it. "Granddaughter," he said, "when was the last time you were near a news terminal? Not that those are to be entirely trusted, either."

She laughed. "Grandsire, you're so paranoid?"

He laughed at her too, shaking that head of shaggy silver-shot hair. "Consider it one of the side effects of venerable old age. But what have you to base the statement on, except rumor?"

She rolled her eyes again. He was in one of his pedantic moods tonight. "It's all we've got, at the moment."

"But not necessarily better than nothing," he said. "I have lived a long time, Granddaughter, and I—"

"—have seen many things," she said in unison with him: mockery, though not entirely unkind. "All right, then, you old fortune-teller, you old stargazer. Tell me how the Elements have decreed that events shall fall for the next day or so."

They had walked a short distance away from the common houses over the beaten-down, dusty ground; he looked at her, smiling slightly, and wouldn't answer. They kept walking into the cool of the growing dusk, in the general direction of the security fence.

He stopped, and she did too, and together they looked toward the low, dimly seen line of the hills twenty miles away. "What a lovely evening," she said, "even down here in the heat."

189

"Yes, it is," he said. His eyes were raised higher, to where a bright-burning point of light hung over the hills: Erivin, the only other planet in the system besides Sammethe, closer to the primary than Sammethe was, and its evening star at this time of year.

"The last evening, for me."

She looked at him, wondering what he meant. "Oh, Grandfather! Don't tell me your heart has been paining you again."

"Not at all."

"And the Klingons aren't going to come back! They've been beaten. Everything is going to be all right now."

"Is it."

She looked into his face, confused.

"Granddaughter," he said, "tomorrow everything changes. Tomorrow is the day our status shifts. And I do not know if I will survive it."

"What?"

He patted the hand which lay over his, and walked her on a little ways. "When I was in Grand Fleet, on outworld patrol, in the ancient days," Mijne's grandfather said, "I saw how our ground ancillaries behaved when things needed to be repaired in a hurry. I grant you, it's hard to see the port well from here, especially the way they keep opaquing the fence during the day. But they have the fence on automatic timing now, and they've misjudged the time of twilight, which is why we can see that as well as we can. Just look at it."

They gazed out toward the port facilities. The landing surface was all pockmarked with holes and craters and huge long gashes gouged out by phaser blasts.

"Tomorrow," Mijne's grandsire said, "we'll be told to go out there and start repairing that. Or else we'll wind up as 'replacements' for other automatics around the base which were damaged and cannot be repaired. We will prove our loyalty by faithfully serving those who have oppressed us."

He grinned. The grin was feral. Mijne thought she had never seen such a ferocious look on anyone, and she was certainly at a loss to see it on her old grandsire, who had spent her childhood spoiling her and giving her treats, and whose voice she had never heard raised.

"Oppressed us?" she said. "Grandfather, you're——" She wouldn't quite say "mad."

"Oh, come, Granddaughter, surely you don't believe they rounded us all up and brought us here to *protect* us!"

"But they said——"

"Of course they did. Free, though, and in our homes, we can't be controlled: with the planet going about its business as usual, there are too many ways we threaten this base's security. For we're mostly Ship-Clan folk, aren't we?—not really to be trusted: different from other Rihannsu, as they like to think, another breed, possibly disloyal. So they distrust us from the start. But also, our world's in a bad spot. We are a long way from the hearth of the Empire,

191

and the Empire would hate to see Sannethe's privately owned shipbuilding facilities falling into the Klingons' hands, while the employees are running around free in the neighborhood, available to be simply swept up and put to work for the Empire's enemies. So instead, the government rounds us all up, the whole workforce of this planet which really has no other industry worth speaking of, and puts us where it can keep an eye on us, while this attack is handled, and the government thinks about what it wants us to build for them . . . never mind what our industry cooperative thinks. Should it look as if the Klingons might somehow get the upper hand here, well . . . someone can make sure that this particular highly skilled workforce is never taken by them as slave labor."

"And a good thing, too! I would die rather than be a Klingon's slave, or any being's!"

"Quite right," her grandfather said. "Quite right. But wouldn't you rather be free to make that choice for yourself, Granddaughter . . . rather than have it made for you?"

She stared at him.

He kept walking gently along. "Well, if we are lucky, it may not come to that. The military may be telling the truth for once, or some of it. Though I doubt it. Sooner or later, though, we'll come to the real reason they've put us here. We will be forced to start work at the base. After that, they will find other work for us to do—either shipbuilding again, on their terms and pay—if any pay at all—or something less pleasant, maybe not even on this planet. And our durance will not end until this not-yet-declared war ends . . . and maybe not even then." He raised his eyebrows.

He was so calm and matter-of-fact about all this that, to Mijne's horror, she was beginning to believe him. "But—I don't see what we can do," she said at last. "They are the government."

"We are Rihannsu," her grandfather said. "We can refuse!"

She stared at him, fearful. "But our duty—"

"Is not to follow stupid orders blindly," her grandfather said fiercely. "Or orders which blithely destroy the freedom our long-ago ancestors brought us here to enjoy at such cost to themselves, after they in turn refused to be other than they were. How should we have become so craven as to acquiesce to our own enslavement? Our government has no such rights over us, of internment, of forced labor. And yes, they will say, now and afterward, it was an emergency, we are fighting for our lives, we will make it up to you later, all your rights will be restored to you!" He gave her an ironic look. "Do you believe that?"

To her horror, Mijne found she didn't. In the last few years she had become troubled by some of the things she saw on the news channels, reports from the outworlds of mass arrests, "security problems," purges of local governments. Then, over the last year, she had seen few such reports, almost none. At first she had thought, *Good, things are quieting down.* But then a small voice had started to say, in the back of her mind, *Are they really? Or are the news services simply not telling these stories anymore? And if not, why not?*

"This system and others like it will shortly be the front line of a war," her grandfather said softly. "And we can only hope that others in the other colony worlds have not yet forgotten how to die for what they believe in." He let out a long breath. "For that is what we will have to do now."

" 'We'—"

"I am a grandson and a twice- and three-times great-grandson of engineers," her grandfather said, stopping now, looking up at that evening star as it slid toward its setting. "Our ancestors and their families left safety, in the ancient days, to bring the rest of our people here. We risked our lives to do it. We died with the ships that died, and in some of the ships that didn't. Now it looks like some of us will have to die again."

His voice was curiously calm. Now it even began to sound amused. "But not in vain, I think, for the Empire's own greed has sown the seeds of what will now begin to happen. It wasn't enough for them to tax us for the privilege, when we desired to spread out into the new worlds discovered after ch'Rihan and ch'Havran were settled. They sited the ship-building facilities on the new outworlds, and made us pay for those too: they made us staff them locally, and pay the staff ourselves." He smiled. "And then, when the exploration ships our more recent ancestors built in turn found new, livable worlds, they taxed us for landing and living on those as well: and those colonists in turn had to pay for and run the new shipbuilding facilities established on the second- and third-generation worlds. Did they never think what they were doing?"

"Grandsire—"

"Mijne, listen, just this once. Greed blinded them: or else the Elements did. The Empire forced the tools of our future independence into our hands . . . and then made them all the more precious to us by forcing us to pay for them, yet withholding true ownership." That feral grin appeared again. "What people need to see at all costs is that we are not powerless . . . *for we are still holding the tools.*"

"To do what?"

"We will have to ask our people, and find out," her grandfather said. "Meanwhile . . ."

He stood still and silent for a few moments more, while Mijne shook in the growing cold.

"One can always say no," he said, as the evening star winked out behind the hills, and the fence went opaque again.

The next morning they were all called together for the usual morning mass meeting in which duties and details were announced. The base commander himself was there. "Considerable damage has been done by yesterday's Klingon attack to base facilities," the commander said. "Immediate repairs must be begun on the landing pans; repair cradles, and cranes if we are to carry the attack to them effectively, or repulse the next one." People looked at each other dubiously. *"Next one"?* The word had gone out that this had been a victory, that the invaders had been driven off, and the rumors had gone on to add that within a few days everyone would be able to go home and pick up their lives where they had left off. "To facilitate this goal, by order of the Empire, work crews will now be formed from the camp's population, consisting of everyone between ages sixteen and one hundred fifty. You are required to form up in groups of one hundred, by registration numbers. Officers will be detailed to each group to describe your duties and work hours. When a project is finished, your officer will inform you of the next project to be begun. Starting with these numbers—"

There was some muttering among the great crowd, but it was muted. The officer seemed not to pay any attention to it, merely kept reading his numbers. The crowd, like a live thing, hesitated, then started to drift apart, fragmenting itself.

One fragment, though, moved through it, in a straightforward direction very unlike the uncertain motion of everyone else. He made his way out of the crowd, clear of the other people, and stepped out onto the bare concrete, stepped out of it, toward the officer. The officer, looking up and seeing him, stopped, puzzled.

The old man drew himself up quite straight, quite tall. In a voice sharp and carrying as the report of a disruptor bolt, he said:

"I will not serve!"

The crowd fell deadly silent.

Mijne blanched as the officer lowered his padd and stared at her grandsire. *He's a hundred and ninety, he doesn't have to serve, Grandsire, what are you*— "Grandsire!"

The officer looked at her grandfather in apparent bemusement. "I beg your pardon?"

"I said," her grandsire said courteously, as if anyone within a half mile could have failed to hear him, *"I will not serve!"*

The officer looked at him. Then he looked at one of the security people off to one side, and muttered something.

The security man lifted his disruptor and fired.

The scream of sound hit Mijne's grandsire, and he went down like a felled tree.

She ran to him, fell to her knees beside him. Between neck and knees he was one great welter of blood and blasted flesh. Her grandsire looked at her with eyes clear with shock. "Did he hear me?" he said.

"He heard you," she said, weeping.

Her grandsire stopped breathing. Unbelieving, Mijne looked up, looked around. All that great crowd looked at what had happened . . . then slowly,

197

slowly began to drift apart again, into groups.

Mijne got up and walked back among them, only very slowly getting control of the sobs that were tearing at her. After a while she managed it. She went to the group she was supposed to be with, and did the work they were given, filling blast craters with rubble; and that night they all went back to their common houses, and a great silence fell with the dark.

But in it, here and there, very faintly, in the depths of night, in Mijne's mind and in many another, a whisper stirred, slowly beginning to look for ways to speak itself in action:

I will not serve . . . !

Arrhae's meeting turned out to consist of three dreary hours of procedural wrangling among the negotiators, during which the observers' and delegates' opinions were neither solicited nor (clearly) desired. On one level, Arrhae didn't mind; she was glad enough to have time to turn over in her mind this new turn of events and what to do about it, though it was a pain to have to appear, at the same time, as if she were paying attention to the mind-numbing arguments of the negotiators about how the parts of the demand to the Federation should be rephrased. When midmeal break came round, it came not a second too soon for Arrhae, and she was all too glad to slip back to her suite for a bite to eat by herself.

Ffairrl appeared and began to fuss over her, and Arrhae suffered it for a few minutes, letting him bring her a cup of ale and a small plate of savory biscuits, but nothing more. "Lady," Ffairrl said, sounding rather desperate, *"Deihu,* they will think I am not serving you well!"

"If you give me another midmeal like yesterday," Arrhae said, "you will have to serve me by rolling me down the hall on a handtruck!" Though now she would be wondering who *his* "they" were. Did the Intelligence people browbeat even the poor servants? *Well, and why would they not? They tried it with me.* But to what purpose? One more question to which she was not likely to get an answer any time soon. . . . And then the door signal went off.

Arrhae looked up at the clock on the nearby table with some indignation. It was nowhere near the end of the midmeal break yet. *"Now what?"* she said, and then thought, *Ah, the package.* . . . Ffairrl, with a nervous look, headed for the door.

It opened . . . and Arrhae saw who stood there, and slowly got up.

A slim, slight young man, a handsome dark-visaged young man hardly much taller than she was, in Fleet uniform, with a cheerful and anticipatory look on his face: Nveid. Nveid tr'AAnikh. The last time Arrhae had seen him, he had been following her while she did her shopping. Initially she'd thought he might have been following her for her looks. That did happen occasionally, for she was unusually good-looking by Rihannsu standards, that having been one element of her cover—her old double-agent master having been widely assumed to have originally bought her for other purposes than household work. But that had not been the reason, and Arrhae had begun to suspect that tr'AAnikh was possibly with one of the Intelligence services . . . until she found out how wrong she had been about that, too.

Now Nveid stepped into her suite and bowed to her . . . a breath's worth, then up again, jaunty, like a suitor who thinks his suit is going to go well and doesn't see the need to be overly formal. "Noble *Deihu*," Nveid said, "I had to see you."

"I am not at all sure the need is reciprocal," Arrhae said, in as hard a voice as she could manage. "Tr'AAnikh, how *dare* you come here? I thought you would have understood after our last encounter that I do not welcome your attentions." This was true, though not for the reasons any listener might suspect. *What is he doing here?* she thought. The brief conversation they'd had in i'Ramnau some weeks ago—though it felt more like half a lifetime now—had suggested that his family might have been under suspicion because they had kin on *Bloodwing. Gorget* was the last place she would have expected to see him.

"I am in attendance on my mother's sister-cousin, the *Deihu* Odirne t'Melanth," he said. "I was seconded to her service a tenday ago, when the mission began to be assembled." Nveid stepped closer to Arrhae, and smiled. "She has found my services invaluable, she says . . ."

The verb *mnhain'he* had the same possibilities for double entendre attached to it that the word *service* had in Anglish, and many more: and Arrhae was not amused by the implications. "Insolence!" Arrhae said. "You are not welcome, I tell you. Go away!"

He stepped still closer. "I did not believe you when you told me that the last time," Nveid said. "And when I heard you were here, I knew it was the Elements themselves that had ordained it so. Fire will have its way, Arrhae, the fire of hearts. . . ."

He was moving closer. Arrhae was slightly alarmed, but more bemused by the poor-quality romantic rhetoric, like something off of the less well subsidized public entertainment channels . . . and more bemused still because there was no reasonable justification for it on his side, not after a total of ten minutes' conversation two tendays ago, and no justification whatsoever on hers. "We burn in the same conflagration," Nveid said, right in front of her now, reaching out to her, taking her by the upper arms. "You denied it then because you were but a poor servant, and could not follow your heart. But now you are noble, now you can avouch your true desires without fear. . . ."

Oh, come on now, Arrhae thought. *What is he at . . . ?!*

He pulled her to him. For a second she was too amazed to struggle, and he put his lips down by her ear and actually nuzzled her.

"The Ship-Clans are rising," he quickly whispered, so softly that even she could hardly hear it. "Bear the winged one the news."

And then he pulled away a little, looked her in the astonished eyes . . . and leaning in, he kissed her, quite, quite hard.

Arrhae's eyes widened at what she felt. What happened after that was sheer reflex. Nveid went flying through the air and fetched up hard, *bang*, against the wall near the door, more or less sitting on the floor and looking dazed, with reason. Arrhae stood there, breathing hard, and staring at him . . . and thinking, *Did I see him wink at me? Did he actually wink??* Rihannsu had that gesture in common with Terrans, but Arrhae wasn't entirely sure that he hadn't simply had something in his eye.

She turned around to find the steward standing there with a disruptor in his hand. *Now where did he get that?* Arrhae thought. *Is he some kind of undercover security guard?* But whether he was or not, she was in no mood for any more surprises. "You're a little late with that, aren't you, Ffairrl?" Arrhae said. "Not that it matters. Put it away, you idiot; he's no threat."

Ffairrl stuck the weapon in his apron pocket, and the haste and clumsiness with which he did it suggested to Arrhae that he had nothing to do with any security contingent—or was acting superbly. *Either way, I hope he put the safety back on . . . !* "Noble lady, shouldn't I call the guards?" Ffairrl said.

RIHANNSU: SWORDHUNT

"For *this?*" Arrhae said, turning to regard Nveid again. "Hardly."

She stepped over to the buffet sideboard, picked up the pitcher that was always there, went straight back to Nveid and upended the pitcher over him. "There's water for your 'fire,' " she said, and chucked the pitcher over her shoulder. There was a crash as it broke on something, possibly that expensive glass-slab table in the middle of the room: she didn't bother to look. "Beware how you invoke an Element in someone else's name when it's not there, you young fool. I intend to have words with your lady about this: we'll see how she likes it that her staff are running around in the corridors like *hieth* in heat, accosting their betters!"

He got up, and made a rather pitiful attempt to put himself right, dripping as he was. "Noble lady—"

"Not another word," Arrhae said. *"Out!"*

He went. The door closed, and Arrhae stood there and breathed out, wondering what in the names of Earth and, yes, Fire, were going to happen next.

Doubtless I'll find out, she thought. *Meanwhile I have other problems....*

"I must go wash my mouth out," Arrhae said, in a tone of voice she hoped was rich with disgust. "As for you, Ffairrl, not a word of this to anyone, otherwise it'll be all over the mission in a *stai* ... and if I hear about it so, it'll be *your* hide I take the strips off, no one else's."

"No, noble *Deihu,* of course not, great lady ..."
Arrhae paid him no more mind. She took herself

203

off to the great bathroom, ran a great deal of water in the highbasin, found a toothscrub, and went to work.

She spent a good while at it—long enough, she thought, to bore anyone who might be watching. And when Arrhae finally turned away from the sink, having run a finger once over her gums in front as if afraid they might have been hurt by the violence and intrusiveness of Nveid's kiss, she was quite sure that no one had seen her remove the tiny square of silicon which she had squirreled away between gum and cheek just after she threw Nveid at the wall.

What a lot of reading I will have to do this evening, Arrhae thought.

The first part of it she did after the day's sessions were over. The "package" t'Radaik had promised her, the data chip, was waiting for her in a little slipskin envelope on the somewhat-scratched glass table when Arrhae came back from the afternoon session. She ate in, that evening, rather than going to the inevitable buffet with the rest of the senior members of the mission, and munched her wafers and *their* at the desk in the luxurious little office, sipping berry wine the while.

The data from t'Radaik's chip was all dry stuff on the surface, seeming to have to do with ship movements and materiel movements on ch'Rihan and ch'Havran: it suggested a great reshuffling of resources in the part of the Empire nearest the Neutral Zone. *True or false?* Arrhae wondered. Surface meanings could be deceptive: there was probably coded content buried in this text, and if it genuinely was sourced from a Federation deep-cover agent like herself, the people who would accompany the Starfleet forces to the negotiations would be equipped to extract it. There was no use her trying her own ciphers on it: even if they had been brand new, which they weren't, they would not be the same as another agent's.

All I can do is pass this on to McCoy as instructed, Arrhae thought. *But not without warning him that the information in it's been compromised . . . or fabricated. It's as I told t'Radaik; there is likely enough a bombshell hidden in this somewhere.*

And as for the rest of my reading . . .

She would have to wait for that: but not too much longer . . . it was late. Ffairrl came in from his little butler's-cupboard room, looked at the empty plate and cup, and said, *"Llhei Deihu,* can I get you anything else?"

No answer to this question ever suited this man but yes. "O Elements, have pity on me," Arrhae said. "Ffairrl, all right, give me some bread and some ale, and for something hot, a bowl of *hehfan* broth. Without the dumplings, thank you. And then do go; there's nothing more to be done tonight, as I flatly refuse to eat anything further."

He went away to make the broth. *What I would like to know is why they're so sure McCoy will be here,* Arrhae thought. *Unless they have somehow discovered that he had that chemical Rihannsu-*

comprehension procedure, *and will be brought along as an extra, "covert" translator: for besides the usual Universal Translator links, there will almost certainly be a live language specialist with them as well.*

And there was always the possibility that, as t'Radaik had implied, they might have someone on *Bloodwing* who had been in touch with McCoy, or someone else on *Enterprise*, and knew where he was going to be. That too was something she was going to have to warn McCoy of. *At least I have the opportunity . . . which Intelligence itself has given me.*

And which they may be hoping to use to find some evidence that I am a double agent. . . .

Ffairrl came in with the bread and soup and ale, and Arrhae thanked him and bade him good night.

"Lady," Ffairrl said somewhat nervously, "should that gentleman return . . .?"

She raised her eyebrows at him. "Did you replace that pitcher?" she said.

He gave her the slightest smile. "Yes, noble *Deihu.*"

"Then that's all I'm likely to need. Go you now, and sleep well."

"Yes, lady," Ffairrl said, and went out; and Arrhae heard the door lock behind him as it shut.

She drank her soup, and drank her ale, and nibbled at the bread while she finished her reading. Then Arrhae shut the computer down, with a yawn not entirely feigned, went to the clothespress in the main room, and pulled out her carrybag. She went through it until she came up with a bottle of the *dheitain*-wood bath oil she favored; and casually she also took out of it her own rather old and crude little pad-scriber, which she had brought from i'Ramnau with her, and had already taken along to one or two of the daily meetings. The excuse was that she was used to it, and liked it, and did not need newer equipment—at least, that would be the excuse if anyone queried her about it. Like Gurrhim tr'Siedhri, Arrhae also had the potential excuse of eccentricity, which others would expect from her, and mock her for behind her back as they mocked tr'Siedhri for holding forth endlessly about the virtues of life on the land, calling him "farmer Gurri" behind his back. *They'll call me hru'hfe,* Arrhae thought, *and laugh . . . until I catch one of them at it. That* was a slightly chilling thought: for *mnhei'sahe* dictated a certain kind of response should that happen.

For the time being, though, Arrhae wasn't going to worry about it. She hoped the eccentricity would be enough to disguise the important thing about having this scriber with her: that she knew it was not bugged.

She straightened up, yawned and stretched again, and headed for the bathroom, dropping the scriber on the table by the bathroom's door, within sight of the big bath. Then Arrhae began testing the plumbing most thoroughly.

The scriber was not out of her sight all during the bath, though Arrhae hoped that fact would pass unremarked by any watcher. When she got out at last, rather wrinkled but very clean indeed, Arrhae left it where it was while she went off to make herself a final cup of herbdraft. With it she sat down in one of the biggest of the big comfortable chairs, watching the stars pour silently by the huge windows. A long while she sat, composing in her mind, sipping the draft until long after it was cold.

At last she got up, put the cup on the sideboard, and started preparing to retire. Arrhae moved gently about the suite, shutting off the lights, picking up the scriber absently and dropping it on the table near the couch.

Then she slipped in under the sleeping silks and waved the last light off. A good while, Arrhae lay there, listening hard, though she knew she would hear nothing; those who listened to her were most unlikely to betray themselves.

It must be long enough now, she thought. Very softly, in the dark, Arrhae reached out and pulled the scriber under the covers . . . then pulled the covers up over her head. As she had done many a night when she was still a *hru'hfe*, she activated the scriber by feel alone, her knowledgeable fingers easily managing the keying of its silent pads in the dark. When the light of its tiny strip of faint-lit screen began to glow, Arrhae slipped Nveid's little scrap of a chip onto the reader pad, and started to read.

Much later, in the blackness, Arrhae put another

chip onto the pad, and began to type . . . smiling all the while.

Jim came into Main Briefing the next morning to find that Ael was there early, watching Scotty and K's't'lk put the final touches on the bones of their scheduled briefing to the science staff on their progress with the "safing" of the Sunseed routines. "Did you rest well, Commander?" Jim said, standing behind her and looking at the hologram she was examining.

"Not too well," said Ael. "But any rest which does not involve being shot at is a good one, I suppose." She turned her attention back to the image currently playing itself out over the center of the table. It was a holographic display of an eclipse of Earth's sun: a particularly splendid one, the primary's corona licking and writhing away from the obscured disk of the photosphere like the wind-rippled mane of some furious and glorious beast.

Jim had seen this particular image before, at the Academy, and afterward occasionally elsewhere. "2218?" he said to Scotty.

"Aye, that's the one," Scotty said, not looking up from his work at the table computer for the moment.

Ael glanced from it to Jim. "It is a great wonder," she said.

"We're more or less used to it now," Jim said. "It happens with some frequency."

Ael laughed, one of those small nearly inaudible

breaths of humor that Jim had nearly forgotten the sound of. "Certainly, though, you have considered how astronomically unlikely such an exact fit of the apparent size of star and moon, as seen from Earth, must be." She gazed at the image again. "I thought, when I saw it for the first time, that the image had been taken by some space vessel or satellite specifically positioned for the purpose."

"No," Jim said. "It just came that way."

She gave him an amused and extremely skeptical look. "You truly believe that this is a coincidence?"

"The universe has seen stranger ones," Jim said.

Ael raised her eyebrows at him, leaning back in the seat. "Perhaps. Though I should like to discuss the statistical realities of the situation with Spock someday: doubtless even in his dry way he might cast light on the provenance of this miracle which he might not otherwise intend."

Jim wasn't sure what to make of that idea. "But there are those of my people who would have taken such an apparition in our own skies as an explicit message from the Powers," Ael said. "An invitation to venture out and discover what it was that had engineered such a spectacular and transient terror. Or simply a message that so colossal a coincidence could not have simply happened: that it was indeed *made*, and that there were makers."

Jim nodded. "Oh, we have our own people who think that the Preservers or some other of the 'seeding' species passed through fifty thousand years or so ago, and nudged the moon just enough in its orbit to produce the effect." He shrugged. "There's no proof of it, naturally. The moon does have some microscopic orbital 'wobbles' that can't be accounted for by its interactions with the Earth and the sun; but as for what causes them—" He shrugged.

"But meanwhile," Ael said, "the wonder remains. And may yet do us good, for worlds used to eclipses even without such a perfect fit tend to be further ahead in research on coronal science than others. Earth being one of them."

Scotty smiled. "Flattery will get you everywhere, lass," he said, not looking up.

Jim looked back at the eclipse, still caught in the repeating loop of the few minutes of totality as seen from the northern Pacific. The so-called Great Eclipse or Fireball Eclipse of 2218 had not only had an unusually long totality, but had coincided with a sunspot maximum, and the solar storm ongoing during the umbra's track across the Earth had produced coronal behavior like nothing ever seen before during an eclipse—outrageous, frightening, enough to give the impression to a viewer that the sun was actually angry, and might do something terminal to its subject worlds. Ael reached out and touched the control to let the image continue through its normal cycle. " . . . It's temporary, at any rate," Jim said. "The moon's getting slowly further away from us. Thirty or thirty-five thousand years from now, and the fit won't be perfect anymore. Nothing but annular eclipses for us, then, until the oscillation stops and the moon's orbit begins closing in again."

"And then what?"

"Then it starts to fall," Jim said, "and tidal forces pull it apart. If we're lucky, Earth ends up with rings. If we're not lucky . . . rings, and most likely a 'cometary winter.' "

Ael looked rueful. "Much later, though, I assume."

"Five or six hundred thousand of our years, give or take a few."

Ael smiled slightly. "Not something we need worry about overmuch, then. Our own concerns lie closer in time."

Jim nodded. The corona licked and lashed in apparent fury; then there came a tremor at the trailing limb, the solar brilliance piercing through the lunar valleys, and the "diamond ring" effect flashed out in full glory, blinding. Ael stood up, gazing at it with the expression of someone faced with an insoluble riddle. "The Elements clearly do have a sense of humor," she said at last, as the sun showed a full blazing crescent of its limb and the corona faded to invisibility. "Unwise of us to ignore it when we see it being displayed. Few are angrier, the poet says, than those who tell a joke and hear no laughter. . . ."

"I don't like to step on anyone's punch lines either," Jim said.

McCoy came in and paused, looking at the eclipse

with a somewhat jaundiced eye. Jim noticed the look. "Problems, Bones?"

"After I saw the recording of the bridge view from yesterday," McCoy said, folding his arms, "I don't much like the look of *that*."

"If you like, Doctor," Spock said as he came in the door, "I will send down to Catering for a pot for you to bang on, to frighten away the wolf."

" 'Wolf'?"

"The one you no doubt feel sure is eating the sun." McCoy's look got slightly sourer as he sat down at the table. "No need to get cute, Mr. Spock. I was merely suggesting that the sun here looks like it was about to pull the same kind of trick 15 Trianguli tried yesterday."

Spock sat down with a slight expression of weariness. "Earth's primary has been known to produce the occasional coronal mass ejection," Spock said, "but normally it does so unassisted."

"Yes, well, 15 isn't likely to try anything like that unassisted *now*, is it, as a result of being tampered with?"

"I would estimate the odds for that as being——"

"Minuscule," Scotty said, and "Vanishingly small," K's't'lk said, and "Statistically insignificant," Spock said, all of them together.

Jim and Ael exchanged a glance. "So much agreement," Jim said, sitting down at the head of the table, "frightens me more than usual. I would move out of the area immediately, except that people are meeting

213

us here. How long till the task force turns up now, Spock?"

"Twelve hours and thirty-three minutes, Captain."

"Thank you."

Other crew began coming in: more Science Department staff, especially several of the more senior astrophysics specialists; and a couple more department heads, including Uhura; and some of Ael's people from *Bloodwing*, among them tr'Keirianh the master engineer and Aidoann t'Khnialmnae, who was doubling as science officer until another more junior crewman should be elevated to that position from the ranks. *Or what they have left of ranks,* Jim thought as the rest of the group filtered in. *I wish I could help her out somehow. Spock's had a look at their automation by now, but there's no substitute for people you can trust....*

"Are we all here?" Jim said. "All right. Anything we need to handle before we get started?"

"One thing, Captain," Uhura said. "Just before I left the bridge, we received a message from the *Sempach*. There have been some schedule changes, it seems. At least a couple of the other ships will be joining us en route to the meeting point at RV Tri, and *Sempach* is now scheduled to rendezvous with us much earlier than the other starships meeting us here: perhaps within the hour. Commodore Danilov sends his compliments, and would like to see you at your earliest convenience."

"Very well," Uhura would have repeated the

commodore's phrasing word for word, which made Jim just slightly nervous: "earliest convenience" might sound polite enough, but it was not-very-secret code for "the minute I arrive, and not a second later." Dan was either very worried about something, or his nose was out of joint, or possibly both. But at least Jim thought he might hear something from Starfleet that they hadn't seen fit to transmit to *Enterprise* on the usual channels. *Or I'm going to get a very long grilling about what happened when we got here. . . .*

"All right," Jim said. "Let's hear what you've got."

K's't'lk tapped at the reader on the table in front of her and brought up her own notes, which she started chiming her way through at speed for the benefit of the Science Department staff on hand. Jim, who had read her preliminary abstract over breakfast and had then immediately resolved never to do such a thing again before the caffeine took, now settled back to wait for the expanded analysis, which would mean more to him than the raw figures.

It took a while, during which he had leisure to worry about Danilov's arrival. "We had been looking for indications of what stars would definitely not be candidates for the Sunseed process," K's't'lk finally said, "so that we could concentrate on the ones that *were*, and could avoid spreading our energies into areas that didn't require them. We feel we don't really need to worry too much about stars that genuinely fall into the 'dwarf' category, because they are the most difficult candidates for induction . . . and indeed, without some genuinely inspired on-the-fly calculations by Mr. Spock, we would not have managed induction at 15 Tri at all. Our conclusion is that dwarf stars are not massive enough to produce coronae with a high enough 'ambient' energy level to induce to produce ion storms using Sunseed. And this includes Sol, which is a genuine nonmarginal dwarf G0: so that's one less thing for the Federation to worry about."

The computer console chirped softly as Scotty worked over it, preparing another display. "However, there are plenty of other non-dwarf stars which have inhabited planets," Scotty said, "the ratio being about one dwarf to four. Based on what we've seen most recently, and on data from the induction that followed the pursuit of *Enterprise, Intrepid,* and *Bloodwing* by the Romulans on the way out of Lev-aeri V, we've managed to cobble together some suggestions for protecting normal main-sequence stars from such inductions. All these are very tentative, of course. . . ."

Scotty killed the eclipse hologram, and the space above the middle of the table started filling up with diagrams and bar charts and pie charts and graphs with jittering lines. "While the coronal mass ejection we produced was a 'standard' one of the halo type with helium alpha," K's't'lk said, "there were interesting variations. One of the most telling phenomena for our purposes was the way the sunspots came up all of a sudden during the induction, completely un-naturally, in a pattern that bears no resemblance whatever to the usual 'butterfly' diagram, the plot of the heliographic latitude of the sunspots versus time. *Much* too much intrusion of the spots into the polar latitudes, suggesting that Sunseed's specific effect on the solar magnetic field is to derange the field in-tensities not above, but *below* local average rates, a 'curdling' effect which spreads all through the lower stellar atmosphere and . . ."

Jim glanced down the table at Ael. She was mak-ing desultory notes on a clipboard-padd, though nothing like the hurried and systematic ones which were being made by tr'Keirianh beside her; and she looked up, caught Jim's glance, and smiled, very slightly, a look of complete bemusement. Jim went back to making his own notes for the moment, which were mostly about things to discuss with Danilov when he got in.

" . . . this being the case, the 'best' candidates, the top of the 'bell curve' and the stars most susceptible to this kind of interference, would be Bw stars with suf-ficiently weak helium lines, or Be stars with the nec-essary 'forbidden' lines in their spectra," K's't'lk was saying. "And fortunately, few of these have planets."

Scotty looked up then. "But most other stellar classes suffer as well. Nearly *all* stars with planets around them, in both Federation and Klingon space, fall on the upper side of the bell curve—probably nearly all the Rihannsu ones as well, though data on that is less certain. We have good astrocartography on the area, but less data on which stellar systems are populated."

"I will gladly help you there," Ael said. "But some of the rumors coming out of the Empire suggest that the data may not be correct for long. Populations are moving, or being moved, or in extreme cases being wiped out, along the fringes of the Imperium. Mostly the latter."

Scotty nodded, pausing to bring up another starmap in the hologram over the table, one which filled with a map of the Neutral Zone boundary and many pulsing points of light. "At any rate, as you see here, nearly every populated star system in which the primary is *not* a dwarf is now a potential target for attacks which at best will make interstellar shipping difficult, and at worst will impair starships' ability to achieve high warp, damage many of them, destroy some of them. This weapon can be moderately easily deployed by an enemy willing to divide his forces sufficiently, going from star to star at warp speeds and leaving bigger and bigger ion storms in his wake."

"There is also a possibility which Mr. Scott and the commander have not mentioned," Spock said, "which is a theoretical one, impossible to test . . . but I would dislike seeing any test made. If too many ion storms of this sort were started at one time by a group of ships in a given area of space, the storm front could possibly gain enough energy to propagate itself for a prolonged period along a wavefront light-minutes or even light-days long. At such energy levels it could propagate into subspace as well, deranging its structure and fabric." Spock looked much more troubled than the mere unpredictability of results could account for. "Such an 'ion firestorm' might render subspace useless for communication, or even incapable of supporting speeds higher than c . . . which would at best mean that there were patches or ruts in subspace where starships could not go. At worst it could mean the end of warp-speed travel in this part of the galaxy, for everyone involved."

Jim looked at Ael. "Do your people know about the possibility of this effect, do you think?"

"I cannot say," Ael said. "But if they find out about it, I make no doubt they would consider its use as a weapon of the 'doomsday' sort."

Jim nodded to Scotty, who killed the displays. "So. Recommendations?"

Scotty looked uneasy. K's't'lk jangled, an unnerved sound, the Hamalki version of nervously clearing one's throat. "Captain," Spock said, "the simplest recommendation for the moment is not under any circumstances to allow Romulans, the party most likely now to use the Sunseed routines, into Federation space in strength. But that may shortly become impossible."

"And if they *do* get in?"

The engineer and the Hamalki looked at Jim

rather bleakly. "I'd prevent that if I could," K's't'lk said. "For the time being."

"Hope springs eternal," Scotty said, smiling at K's't'lk a little grimly. "But Captain, the next recommendation is to start building solar orbiting facilities in every inhabited star system, heavily shielded for defense, carrying complements of photon torpedoes and lasers capable of disrupting any attacking ship's attempts to 'seed' a corona."

"That would take years!" McCoy said.

"Aye," Scotty said. "Years we haven't got. And any mobile platform can be destroyed if you bring enough power to bear."

" 'For the time being,' though," McCoy said, looking over at K's't'lk. "I thought you were also looking for 'remote solutions.' Ways to handle this problem without having to chase around all over space. Orbital stations aren't all that remote."

Scotty and K's't'lk threw each other a regretful glance. "No," K's't'lk said. "They'd be an interim solution at best. Remote solutions are a lot harder, because we're still trying to write equations that will adequately express the problem. Mr. Spock has had a run at this . . ."

McCoy glanced over at Spock. "And you haven't solved it already? You mean you hit a problem and *bounced*?" The look in his eye was not entirely regret.

"Doctor," Spock said, "one must have a complete question before one can find answers. Even in your slightly chaotic science, you would not treat a patient before he had been properly diagnosed. In this situation—"

"Slightly chaotic—?!"

"—partial solutions are worse than none at all. The only way to affect stars remotely, without directly applying energy to them via phasers, photon torpedoes, and other such mechanical methods, is to alter the structure of the medium in which they are immersed—space and subspace themselves."

"It's not easy," K's't'lk said, her chiming becoming more complex, a toccata scaling up in sixths. "Leaving out the use of supraphysical instrumentalities like elective mass to alter the shape of space——"

"You'd *better* leave them out," Jim said sharply. "No messing around with my engines this time, Commander! We've got too much trouble in this reality to go getting ourselves immersed in some other one."

K's't'lk contrived to look faintly embarrassed—a good trick for someone with no facial features to speak of, except all those hot blue eyes. "I did promise, Captain," K's't'lk said. Jim settled back and tried not to look too stern. "At any rate, Sc'tty and I have been investigating some other possibilities for ways to stop a Sunseed induction. Some of them have to do with stellar 'diagnostic' techniques which go back a ways. The most promising of these involves atomic resonance spectrometry, and evaluation of the acoustic oscillation of a given star, with an eye to bending subspace so that it alters the frequency of that oscillation, changing the solar mag-

221

netic field's influence on the corona and derailing the Sunseed effect that way—"

McCoy looked up suddenly. "Wait a minute. 'Acoustic'? As in sound? You mean the whole thing—a whole star, a sun, *vibrates*?"

"Oscillates, yes, indeed, Doctor. Like a plucked string. As for sound, naturally you could not hear it in vacuum, there being no medium to transmit it, but the acoustic vibration it remains nonetheless. Possibly the 'music of the spheres' your people used to talk about."

"Now, hold on just a second—"

"But even your poets mention stars singing. I'd thought perhaps they were unusually perceptive of stellar physics in either the acoustical or nonphysical mode . . ."

"Uh," McCoy said.

"Give up while there's still time, Bones," Jim said softly, and smiled.

"You mean they weren't? Then they were inspired," K's't'lk said. "But in any case, the oscillation is a phenomenon that has been known for centuries, even among your own people. Your astrophysicists have been using it for some time to analyze the general health of your stars, and to predict their moods."

"Commander," Spock said, looking interested, "this line of inquiry was not mentioned in this morning's précis . . ."

"No. Scotty came up with it on the way here in the lift, and we've been discussing it since."

"It is a fascinating concept," Spock said, folding his hands, steepling the fingers. "A star treated in such a manner might be made to produce oscillations which would cancel out those induced by the Sunseed routines, along the 'canceling sines' principle."

Scotty looked uncertain. "I follow you, Mr. Spock, but you've still got the problem of the complexity of the waves induced in the first place: they're not so simple as sines, either in the original generation or the way they interact with one another after induction. It's not one standing wave you'd have to cancel, but ripple after ripple in the solar 'pond,' all washing through one another and altering one another's frequencies and amplitudes. And then there's the matter of how the star's chromosphere reacts to the stress. Depending on the class of the star and the balance of the various heavy metals——"

"I grant the validity of the concern," Spock said, "but more to the point is the manner in which subspace is caused to make this alteration in the star's acoustical 'body.' Again one comes up against the logistical difficulties attendant on needing to build, deploy, and defend a mobile field generator of some kind."

Scotty raised his eyebrows, and bent over the computer console again, which chirped softly as he started doing some calculations. "It's possible that such a generator might not actually have to be near the star," Scotty said, "if you were using subspace to transmit the information about how subspace was itself going to be altered elsewhere. Like throwing a rock into the water. The ripples start here, but they wind up there . . ."

"That would take quite a while," K's't'lk said, her chiming going minor-key. "Unless you feel like invoking the equivalence heresy, and I'm not sure that's appropriate with our present data. Now if, instead, you altered subspace string structure by using the Gott III hypothesis to——"

"Sorry, K's't'lk, you lost me," Jim said. "'Heresy'? Kind of an odd term to come up in a discussion of astrophysics . . ."

"Oh, it's not just astrophysics, Captain," K's't'lk said, "it's physics in general. The simplest way to explain the heresy—if indeed it is one: the tests of the theory have all been equivocal—would be as an outgrowth of those parts of quantum theory which suggest that it's possible to make a particle over *there* do something by doing something to a particle over *here* . . . the effect propagating to the distant one in some way we don't understand. Early versions of the heresy mostly appeared because of the limitations of physics in earlier times, when science hadn't yet come to understand as much as we do now about the nature of subspace and its complex relationship with some of the more exotic subatomic particles. Now we're a little better informed——"

"A wee bit," Scotty said, looking as if the information wasn't enough for *him*. He hit a control on the computer to save the calculations he had just done, and it chittered softly in response.

"But there are still large areas where we're unsure of what's going on, especially as regards the curvatures of subspace, whether those curvatures are isotropic, or permanently isotropic . . ." K's't'lk waved a couple of forelegs. "And the equivalence heresy springs from one of these. Some theoreticians have suggested that, if small-scale shifts like those of one quark affecting another at a distance can happen, then larger-scale ones happen too . . . and we should be able to *cause* them to happen. If cause is the right word, when something is done to a particle, or atom, or molecule here, and another particle does the same without it being even slightly clear *why*."

"Sounds like magic to me," said McCoy.

"But not to me, sirs and ladies," said Master Engineer tr'Keirianh suddenly, and everyone turned to look, even Ael. "The mathematics of our physics would suggest that such could happen. But our physics also has an ethical mode which suggests that the Elements are one in Their nature, straight through the universality of being . . . and there is no way such 'plenum shifts' could *not* happen: 'as at the heart of being, so at the fringes and out to the Void.'" He frowned a little, his look for the moment closely matching Scotty's. "I will agree, the mathematics involved is thorny. Finding a way to describe accurately what we think might be happening . . ." He shrugged, a purely human gesture, and Jim looked at the graying hair and the lined face and suddenly, he couldn't tell why, conceived a liking for this man. "It is challenging. And also disturbing."

K's't'lk chimed soft agreement. "Yes," she said. "It has been very controversial among my people's physicists: there have been some unplanned reembodiments over the issue."

Knowing what he knew about the Hamalki life-cycle, Jim wasn't sure whether this translated exactly as "suicides." He hoped it didn't. "K's't'lk," he said, getting up and walking around the table to where she sat, "how do you mean 'controversial' exactly? Your people have been rewriting physics cheerfully for centuries, on the local scale anyway . . . something that other physicists find distressing, but that doesn't seem to bother you people in the slightest. But *this* is 'controversial'?" He shook his head. "After all, you could just do it if you wanted to."

"If," K's't'lk said, looking up at him. "Of course we could. But our physics, like that of the Rihannsu, includes an ethical mode as well as a strictly mathematical one. The math tells you how . . . and the ethics tell you whether you *should*. In this case . . ." She jangled a little, an uneasy sound. "If equivalences on this scale are indeed possible, they might break the unwritten 'first law of space.'"

"You mean there are *written* ones?" McCoy said, with his eyebrows up.

"In the form of the clearly expressed physical behavior of the universe, of course there are," K's't'lk said. " 'Don't let go of a hammer above your feet while standing over a gravity well. Don't breathe vacuum.' How large does the print have to be?" She chimed laughter. "But Doctor, this is something else. The inferred, inherent right of being to be *otherwise.*"

"That I understand," McCoy said emphatically.

"You may," Jim said, "but now *I'm* lost?"

Scotty folded his arms and leaned on them. "Captain," he said, "have you ever heard the saying 'Time is God's way of keeping everything from happening at once'?" Jim nodded. "Well then," Scotty said, "there's a corollary to that law: Space is God's way of keeping everything from happening in the same place. God or not, space seems to violently resist physical objects coinciding—say by sharing the same volume, like someone beaming into a wall—"

"Doctor," Ael said, concerned, "are you cold?"

"No, Commander," McCoy said. "Not yet, anyway. But thank you."

Jim smiled. "—or by being forced into synchronization in other ways. Some have called it a reaction against the oneness of all matter and energy in the 'ylem' of pre-time, before the Big Bang. Whatever, the general tendency of the universe is presently away from order, toward chaos. That's just entropy. But it can also be expressed in another way: Things don't want to be the same, or stay the same; they want to be different, and get more so."

"No '*Plus ça change, plus c'est la même chose*'...?"

"In life, yes. In this area of physics, no...."

The communicator went. "Bridge to Captain Kirk," said Mr. Mahase's voice from the bridge.

Jim stepped over to the table, hit the comm button. "Kirk here."

"*Sempach* has just dropped out of warp, Captain, and is closing. ETA five minutes."

"Hold that thought," Jim said. "Not the one about *Plus ça change*: the other one. I know you're still feeling your way through this, but we need solutions fast." He looked down the table at Ael. "Commander, would you walk with me briefly?"

She rose and accompanied him out the door. When it closed behind them, Jim said, "Ael, the commodore in command of *Sempach* is likely to have mixed feelings about your crew at large spending any more time aboard *Enterprise*, even as controlled as the circumstances have been. You, and your senior officers, under supervision, I can now justify ... but no one else for the time being. And things may change without warning. I hope you'll understand."

"Captain," Ael said, "I understand better than you think. And I thank you for trusting us so far ... when I have sometimes misstepped in that regard."

Jim nodded; then said, "I should go see the commodore. Spock will assist you with anything you need in the meantime; I'll see you later."

"We will be moving out for the rendezvous point," Ael said, "after the rest of the task force arrives?"

"That's the plan as I know it. If the commodore gives me different news, I'll see that you know about it as soon as possible."

"Very well," Ael said. "I shall be on *Bloodwing* for the time being: with another Federation ship in view, and more coming, my place is with her. Until matters stabilize."

They stepped into the lift together. "Until they do . . ."

"Till then, luck and the Elements attend you," Ael said.

"Thanks," Jim said, thinking, as the lift doors shut, *I hope I don't need it, or them. . . .*

Continued in
Star Trek #96
Honor Blade
Now Available

229

Look for STAR TREK fiction from Pocket Books

Star Trek®: The Original Series

#4 • *Violations* • Susan Wright
#5 • *Incident at Arbuk* • John Gregory Betancourt
#6 • *The Murdered Sun* • Christie Golden
#7 • *Ghost of a Chance* • Mark A. Garland & Charles G. McGraw
#8 • *Cybersong* • S.N. Lewitt
#9 • *Invasion!* #4: *Final Fury* • Dafydd ab Hugh
#10 • *Bless the Beasts* • Karen Haber
#11 • *The Garden* • Melissa Scott
#12 • *Chrysalis* • David Niall Wilson
#13 • *The Black Shore* • Greg Cox
#14 • *Marooned* • Christie Golden
#15 • *Echoes* • Dean Wesley Smith, Kristine Kathryn Rusch & Nina Kiriki Hoffman
#16 • *Seven of Nine* • Christie Golden
#17 • *Death of a Neutron Star* • Eric Kotani
#18 • *Battle Lines* • Dave Galanter & Greg Brodeur

Star Trek®: New Frontier

New Frontier #1–4 Collector's Edition • Peter David
#1 • *House of Cards* • Peter David
#2 • *Into the Void* • Peter David
#3 • *The Two-Front War* • Peter David
#4 • *End Game* • Peter David
#5 • *Martyr* • Peter David
#6 • *Fire on High* • Peter David
The Captain's Table #5 • *Once Burned* • Peter David
Double Helix #5 • *Double or Nothing* • Peter David
#7 • *The Quiet Place* • Peter David
#8 • *Dark Allies* • Peter David
#9-11 • *Excalibur* • Peter David
    #9 • *Requiem*
    #10 • *Renaissance*
    #11 • *Restoration*

Star Trek®: Invasion!

#1 • *First Strike* • Diane Carey
#2 • *The Soldiers of Fear* • Dean Wesley Smith & Kristine Kathryn Rusch

Other Books

KIRK vs. KIRK

STAR TREK®
PRESERVER

A novel by William Shatner
Available now from Pocket Books

PRES